# Contents

1.

2.

3.

4.

5.

6.

7.

8.

9.

10.

11.

12.

13.

14.

15.

16.

17.

18.

19.

20.

21.

22.

# CHAPTER ONE

Only an hour ago, Molly fixed her wild red hair into plaits, and it was already unravelling. 'Ready.' She looked to the floor, composed herself and waited for the word.

Deirdre, her friend from College who was also the director of this audition piece, quietly said in her best director's don't-spook-the-actor voice, 'And action.'

Molly looked up and into the lens, gave it some sizzle and said, 'Sir, spare your threats: The bug which you would fright me with I seek. To me can life be no commodity: The crown and comfort of my life, your favour, I do give lost; for I do feel it gone...'

'Sorry. Sorry. Sorry.' A voice announced from the doorway of the small front room that had been commandeered for the set on which to shoot this masterpiece of a scene.

'Cut,' Deirdre said with a razor-sharp enunciation that would thinly slice a boiled ham.

Molly held out her long arms in a pleading pose. 'Mam? Really?'

Val, Molly's mother, always insisted that Molly call her Mam and not Ma. Ma was common. Val detested all things common. 'Sorry. Sorry. Sorry,' she said again in a way that didn't sound like she was the least bit sorry at all, no matter how many times she said it while placing a tray of fancy triangle-shaped sandwiches down on the side table, 'I just thought you and your friend would like something to eat.' She motioned to the offering like the lady on the shopping channel offering up this week's special sale item.

Deirdre gave the plate of sandwiches a dubious look of nervous suspicion.

Molly asked, 'What's in them?'

'No meat,' said Val, ' if that's what you're wondering.' She gestured again with slightly more emphasis to make a second attempt at the sale of the fancy sandwiches and took on a light encouraging tone. 'Just cheese and lettuce.'

'Cheese?' Deirdre looked at Molly in a milky horror.

'Yes,' said Val, 'I know that you're all vegetarians nowadays.' She unconsciously touched her perfectly tied-back hair.

Molly said, 'Mam, Deirdre is a vegan.'

Val had no idea what that meant. It might be an illness or a religion. She looked at Molly with a perfectly blank expression, like a seasoned poker player raising on a bluff, and ran her hands over her trim hips like a gunslinger feeling for her pistols.

Molly, seeing that her mother had gone into one of her off-earth orbits, said, 'Deirdre doesn't eat anything that is the product or byproduct of an animal.'

'That must be terrible for her,' Val said, deciding it was most probably some religious thing, like the way Muslims and Jews don't eat rashers; she looked again at the fancy cheese and lettuce sandwiches, trying to work out what the offending article might be. 'But there's no meat in them...'

'Cheese...' Deirdre said, like a TV police detective inspector uncovering a small piece of damning evidence.

Val was still at a loss. 'Cheese?'

Deirdre composed herself to give expert evidence at the trial of *the woman with the cheese and lettuce sandwiches*. 'The dairy industry separates mothers from the calves to make them produce milk, and then (she took a big beat for dramatic emphasis) they leave the male calves in a cage to starve to death.'

Val now understood that it was not religion that prevented Deirdre from eating the cheese but solidarity with the baby cows. She felt a sudden wash of shame, like the receiver who unknowingly bought stolen goods at the door from a junkie shoplifter who was shoplifting to feed their habit. Ignorance is no defence from the law. Had she unknowingly been a facilitator in something so horrible? The forced separation of mother and child? The cruel killing of innocent baby cows? She looked again at the plate of evidence stacked against her. 'That's terrible.'

Deirdre entered into her closing arguments. 'Cheese is made with milk,' she said in a tone full of accusation like a well-honed barrister surgically eviscerating the guilty sandwich lady on the stand.

'Of course,' Val said. She'd like to have told Molly's rude friend how to behave in another woman's home, but it was one of the tenets of Val's belief system that visitors to her home are offered hospitality and fancy sandwiches. She asked, 'Would yous like a cup of tea? With no milk?'

'Mam, We're fine. Thanks.' Molly gave her mother the look she started giving her when she got cast in Annie and decided she didn't want her bringing her into the rehearsals. Val was cordoned off to the sidelines to sit with the chaperones who were employed to look after the small army of stage orphans. She nodded. Hurt, of course, but well able for the slings and arrows of motherhood. 'Sounds very good anyway. What you're doing,' she said, 'I never did any Shakespeare myself when I was a working actress.' She smiled at Deirdre and waited for her to ask about her acting career.

But Deirdre didn't budge on it because she wanted to point out to Val that the term *actress* is offensive. She wanted to tell her that one who acts is considered an actor, just as one who practices the law is considered a lawyer. But she didn't say any of that to Val because she thought it would be like arguing with a pigeon.

'Thanks, Mam,' Molly said again with a beat of finality like *we're done here now.*

Val nodded again, making her inglorious exit, taking the rejected offering of fancy cheese and lettuce sandwiches with her.

'Where was I?' Molly asked Deirdre with the swipe of her hand, clearing the atmosphere so that she was once more prepared to enter the scene and stand in a Tudor court arguing for her life.

'For I feel it gone,' Deirdre said.

'Right.' Molly's primal anger of ancient origin heated her blood. She was annoyed at her mother for being her mother, annoyed at herself for being herself.

Deirdre put her finger to her lips like a bad actor, thinking a thought and gesturing to prove it. 'Just wondering … Is it the right monologue for you, Molly?'

Molly stopped and looked around the overly furnished small room like she had been suddenly teleported into an undiscovered country. A wisp of rage flashed across her green eyes. 'It's a great fucking monologue.'

Deirdre got the whiff of cordite and grabbed a foothold on the high ground. 'It's Shakespeare, so that's a given.' She was not about to give way. 'But is it right for you?' She touched her chin thoughtfully and examined Molly the way she'd seen directors examine their actors. She hadn't come to the part of the directing course where they teach student directors how to be superior to all other creatures on the set. Still, she'd been studying up on it in her own time by watching youtube instructional videos, practising different tones of her voice, different faces, poses, gestures and looks. She'd watched the interview of an old director who'd worked in Hollywood, and he gave a piece of advice that stuck with her – *nobody knows anything, so pretend you know everything.*

Molly felt her scalp getting hot and her neck burning under her collar, which was usually a weather warning for an approaching argument. 'I don't follow you'

Deidre continued in her *I know everything* mode, 'I mean, Hermione – she's just had a baby in prison that's been taken from her, and now she's facing execution. It's just.' She took a hard beat for emphasis and looked profoundly into the palm of her hand. 'She's a mother and a wife.' Then, another beat was taken while she looked up into the light as if what she was about to say would change the lives of all the characters in the play forever. 'Are you too young?'

Molly was having none of it. 'I'm nineteen.'

'I know that. But you look younger. A lot younger.'

Molly said, 'Girls were married by fourteen in the Tudor period.'

Deirdre nodded but not in agreement. 'Hermione has been through so much … she would be haggard by it.'

Molly was just about coming to the boil. 'What do you think is the right part for me?'

Deirdre spat it out. 'What about Juliet?'

Molly blew her gasket and waved her fist in the air like a Bolshevik. 'Fucking Juliet! Really? Do you know how many Juliet monologues are being sent into agents? I bet you agents are like – If

I have to watch another Juliet monologue, I'll pluck out my fucking eyeballs!'

Deirdre felt the heat of Molly's creative rage that was passionate enough to fill the stage of a West End theatre. But she could also see a naïvety in her that would be perfect for Juliet. She was sure that if Molly could put herself into one of the monologues of the young star-crossed lover, it would be a perfect fit. She tried again, 'Yes … you're right. Just that … I don't feel you are a Hermione.'

'Isn't that the point?'

'The point?'

'Of acting! Nobody knows what it feels like to have a baby in prison and then have it taken away by force and then be taken for execution by a fucking psychopathic husband. As an actor – you make the journey to the character. The further the character is from you, the better vehicle it is for you to show your talent. It was in the lecture.'

Deirdre was at the same lecture on the art of acting that was given in the college by an old thespian who mostly regaled the young hopefuls with anecdotes of treading the boards opposite various icons whom he referred to on a first-name basis. It was Richard did this, and Elizabeth did that when he was a glorified spear carrier at the Royal Shakespeare Company. He proposed that emerging actors should choose roles that showcase their talents by playing cripples or ugly people.

Molly held her ground. 'C'mon. It's a great fucking monologue for me.'

Deirdre realised that she wasn't going to convince Molly to play to her strengths, and for the hundred euros she was getting for the directing, shooting and editing, she'd tried about as hard as she should. She decided to keep her directorial integrity for another day. 'Right. Yes. Right. Let's do it. And we're rolling.'

Molly felt her hair completely escaping from the plaits and her hot blood rushing through her body like it was trying to murder someone. 'Sir! Spare your threats!'


William Hagan sipped his tea as Val returned to the kitchen with the tray of rejected cheese and lettuce sandwiches, placed them carefully on the table in front of him and waited for his response.

'They look lovely,' he said.

'Apparently not.' She walked away from him to the counter and poured herself a fresh cup of tea. 'Have you heard about this thing about the cows and their babies being taken away from them?'

He shook his head. 'No idea. The internet is full of mad stuff about cows.'

She nodded to the sandwiches. 'You might as well have one if you want.'

He carefully picked up one of the delicate triangles and devoured it in one bite.

She sat at the table, unconsciously wiping away invisible crumbs and watching him eat. 'Sometimes I feel like I'm on another planet.' She looked around the kitchen to see if she recognised it. 'I just brought in some sandwiches. What kind of a home wouldn't offer someone tea and sandwiches? I mean, I know your mother didn't believe in hospitality. What was it she used to say?'

'A favour today is an obligation tomorrow.'

'No. Not that one. The one about charity.'

'Charity is a form of vanity.'

'That one. She was a hard woman.'

'She grew up poor.'

'Nobody was rich, but you try to be hospitable.'

'Well, you know what they say – nil nisi bonum.'

'I never heard of that. What is it?'

'Don't speak ill of the dead.'

'Well, I heard of that.'

'That's where it comes from. The Latin.'

'Listen to you. Latin.'

'It's on the wall in work. I didn't know what it meant either until I asked.'

She flicked her tea towel at an offending thought. 'I'm not speaking ill of your mother. I'm just saying that she was inhospitable.'

'I know. You're right.'

'She didn't even look up from her book the first time I went into your house.'

'That's just how she was when she had her nose in a book. The house could burn down around her. It wasn't personal.'

'She was so rude.'

'Yes. She was very rude.'

'But they say that about the protestants. Rude people.'

There was no defending his mother. Constance Hagan was very blunt, very rude, and very protestant.

Val felt placated. 'God be good to her, anyway.' She blessed herself. 'It was different in my mammy's home.' She sipped her tea, which was still too hot to drink, and left a lipstick mark on the rim of her cup. 'A plate of sandwiches. You'd think I was serving up the head of Saint John the Baptist on a platter – God forgive me.' She blessed herself in two fast slashes of her fingers.

He asked, 'What are they even doing in there?'

'It's called a showreel.'

'A what?'

'They make a recording of their audition pieces to send them out to agents and casting directors. It's the latest thing.'

Val has been involved in drama since Hagan met her thirty years ago, and every time he asks a question about it, he hears something new. 'What about the new headshots?'

'What about them?'

'Does she still need them?'

'Of course.'

He sipped his tea.

She wiped an imaginary spot off the table. 'That other one. Miss, Know-it-all. What's she like? With her put-on South Dublin accent. Please!'

'C'mon now. She's in college. That's the whole point.'

'What point?'

'For students from different backgrounds to mingle.'

'I suppose.'

He saw her going into thought, and nothing good ever comes from Val being quiet. 'What would I know about college? I left school at fifteen.'

She sipped her tea. It was still too hot. 'I actually got accepted into Trinity to do the BA in acting.'

'I know.'

'But I took that part as one of the village girls in The Playboy over in Leeds instead. D'you remember?'

'I do.'

'I only took it because I was also understudying Pegeen Mike, and she was supposed to leave the production halfway through to do a movie.' She sipped her tea again as if the harsh memories were contained in the cup. 'Movie got cancelled. I only got four performances of Pegeen, and everyone said I should have had the part from the start.'

'You did alright.'

'Did I?'

'You had that part of a maid in that movie with Julia Roberts in it, in the same scene with her and everything. Who can say that?'

She thinks about that. 'They cut my line.'

'Because you stole that scene.'

She examines him. She knows he's buttering her up, but he's the only fan she's got; she'll take it.

He says, 'It's a well-known fact that they protect these stars. The only thing that anyone will remember from that scene is the maid who brought in the tea.'

'I shoulda went to London when the movie came out.'

'You should get back out there.'

She sipped more tea. He was touching on her secret fantasy now. He said, 'The Widow Quinn.'

She smiled despite herself.

'You'd be a great Widow Quinn.'

She leaned in and kissed him on the cheek, leaving her lipstick there like a stamp of approval, then walked to the sink and rinsed out her cup. Finished with it and its contents. 'Don't mind me. I think I'm going through the change.' She worked the tea towel in her hands, drying the mug, thinking about Pegeen Mike drying glasses behind the bar and how she'd practised until it became the unconscious act of a young girl who'd grown up behind the bar in a rural shebeen out in the middle of nowhere, in a place where nothing ever happened until the boy who killed his father came in and rocked her world.

'You're only fifty,' he said.

At some point, somewhere around her twenty-fifth birthday, she stopped believing in the eternal hope of *maybe this time* and gave up on her acting career. She was young to throw in the towel. Usually, that absurd hope burns on through midlife. She made a clean start at an ordinary life with an ordinary man. Hagan looked good in his army uniform, and there was something solid and dependable about him. She didn't love him, but she didn't need to love him because he was besotted by her, and that would do just fine. Then she had a baby, and all her terrible ambition was reborn. She became determined that her daughter would succeed where she had failed. 'She used to come to me for all that. I used to get her ready for her auditions.'

'You did. That was great.'

'For years … Everywhere she went, people recognised her. It's the Jam Tart Princess. You know, I said to her a few weeks ago that maybe she could go up for an ad.'

'Yeah?'

'Guess what she said to me?'

'No idea.'

'She tells me that she's not going up for ads. She says no one will take her serious if she does them. Did you ever hear such nonsense? Julia Roberts does ads.'

'Yes. But…' he stopped talking. This was one of those dark back alleys that he knew not to wander into. It's the kind of place he could get mugged.

'But what?'

'Nothing.'

'But what?' She wasn't about to let him turn around and walk away now.

He felt like a fool. All these years married, he can still be lured off the main thoroughfare on his way to school and have his lunch money stolen. He had to cough it up. 'Julie Roberts was famous before she started doing the ads.'

'What has that got to do with it?'

'Molly wants to be taken seriously.'

She turned her back on him and washed out the cup again.

It was time for him to get out of here. 'Anyway, I have to go. Can I take these sandwiches for the lads?'

She answered without looking at him. 'Better than them going in the bin, I suppose.'

'Great.' He started to load the sandwiches into a ziplock bag.

'What are you going to say about them?'

'Say?'

10

She perfectly folded up the tea towel like an officiate conducting a religious ceremony. 'About the sandwiches. Why you have them?'

He shrugged. 'I don't think the lads will care enough to ask. They'll just be happy with them and eat them.'

She draped the tea towel over the handle of the cooker door as if she was showing everyone that this was the proper way to fold it and the proper place for it. When the tea towel was just as she wanted it, she looked at him. 'Well, if they do ask, don't tell them that they weren't good enough for the vegan.'

'They wouldn't even know what that means.' He smiled at her to see if he could get a smile back.

She didn't smile back.

Taking the bag of cheese and coleslaw sandwiches, he kissed her on the cheek. 'Feck the vegan.'

She smiled.

He made his exit.

She poured herself a fresh cup of tea and listened to the scene coming through the walls.

'Proclaimed a strumpet: with modest hatred.'

# CHAPTER TWO

'WE'RE HERE.' HAGAN nudged Frank out of his snooze in the shotgun seat.

Frank rubbed the sleep off his face with both hands. 'Gettin too old for this.'

It was 1:15 a.m. when they arrived at the five-star Mountcharles Hotel to pick up a corpse. The headlights illuminated a saturated red-cheeked rookie Garda standing point duty at the front door in the rain like a statue of misery that came to life when he saw the morgue ambulance pulling up. He trotted through the puddles to the driver's side window, holding his hand on his hat so it wouldn't blow away and said, 'He wants you to use the back door!'

'He?' Hagan asked through the slightly lowered window.

The rookie nodded his head to the hotel entrance. 'The Detective.'

Hagan looked through the curtain of weather into the warm low-lit foyer to see the glaring eyes of a grey-haired suit with a face like a slapped arse peering out at them.

The rookie added, 'You should probably kill the emergency lights,' with a sharp nod back to the hotel as if he was receiving telepathic slaps on the head from his superior officer.

Hagan said, 'You should stand in there out of the weather. People die in this kind of stuff.'

The rookie shivered and stayed diligently saturated in his duty.

The arse-faced detective kept eyeing the ambulance as Hagan drove around to the back of the hotel – with his emergency lights on.

Frank muttered, 'This one is goin to be a pain in the arse. I sense it.'

Frank had been picking up the bodies of the sudden and unexpected dead of Dublin for over thirty years, and he'd developed a keen sense of what jobs would, or would not be, a pain in the arse. Hagan had been sharing the intimate space of the ambulance with him for ten years.

'I was in here before,' Frank said.

'When?'

'Back in the day when it was really fancy in the eighties.'

'No way. The eighties?'

Frank nodded. 'Back when I was a youngfella in the fire brigade. There was a suicide up on the top floor. Young woman. We attended and helped carry her down all the stairs. There was a big rich American in the lobby, the big cigar and all the rest of it, and he shoved a tenner into each of our pockets as we were taking her out.'

Hagan shook his head. 'Wow.'

Frank made a bad attempt at an American accent, '"God bless you guys" he said.'

Hagan buried his grin. 'Amazing.'

Frank added, 'That's back when a tenner was a tenner.'

'Have you still got it?'

'Got what?'

'The tenner.'

'Go fuck yourself.'

Hagan laughed a little.

Frank sniffed and said, 'You smell that?'

The ambulance's lights illuminated a great vine of black wrought iron Victorian pipes that covered the hotel's back wall and fed waste into the two-hundred-year-old sewage system that was overwhelmed by the weather and created a lake of sewage in the laneway leading to the rear entrance.

'That'll clear the sinuses.' Hagan carefully drove through the tight lane and was hit with the nose-pinching stink of hydrogen sulfide.

Frank said, 'You know, ancient mystics used to save up their shite in pots until it was really rancid and then sniff it to get high.'

'Fuck off…'

'True,' Frank raised his hand like he was swearing on the bible in court, 'Saw it on that show Weird and Wonderful.'

'Does be good stuff on that show.'

'Breath easy,' warned Frank. 'We don't want you getting any visions.'

'Hold on,' said Hagan, 'I'm getting one now… I see you buying a round.'

Frank grunted because he didn't drink and thought it was a waste of money.

Ahead of them, another miserable rookie appeared, taking shelter in a doorway where a sign on the wall declared that this door was for STAFF ONLY. Beside that sign was a NO SMOKING sign. Then, a NO BICYCLES sign. Then, a NO LOITERING sign. Then, a sign warning YOU ARE BEING MONITORED BY CCTV.

'Let's see what we have then.' Frank got on with the first piece of safety procedure when visiting scenes of death, putting on black latex gloves.

'Wellies?' Hagan looked at the sewage outside.

'Absolutely.'

They reached behind the seats to retrieve their wellingtons, put them on, grabbed their black rubber long coats and stepped out of the cab into the sewage and the rain. Frank moved quickly to the back of the ambulance, retrieved the fold-up stretcher and a white plastic bodybag and made his way to the staff door where Hagan was talking to the rookie in the corridor. 'Where's the body?'

The rookie was high as a kite from the shite fumes, speaking fast, 'He's up in the kitchen! I'm to bring you right up straight away!' He set off like a trooper on a mission.

Hagan put his hand in the air. 'Hold your horses. First things first,' and retrieved his morgue docketbook from his inside pocket. 'Do we have a name?'

'Garda Grimes.'

'For the deceased?'

'Oh. Hold on.' The rookie consulted his notebook and examined the page like he was reading somcone clse's handwriting, 'Eh … Marco? Marco. Yeah.'

Hagan wrote in his docketbook. 'Does Marco have a second name?'

The rookie shrugged. 'The manager says they have to check with the personnel manager in the morning. He's an agency worker. Apparently. Whatever that means.'

*Whatever that means.* Hagan and Frank shared a look. The bodymen knew it meant a lot of extra paperwork because the term *Agency worker* is the universal code for an immigrant working in the country illegally for a pittance. However, getting an ID for an undocumented foreign national is almost impossible. The Coroner's clerk can spend up to two years working with overseas agencies to identify the deceased and locate a next of kin. During this time, the remains will remain frozen in the morgue. In the end, if identification cannot be made, the bodymen will bring the corpse to the graveyard, where it will be buried without ceremony and given an index number in the pauper's plot.

Frank sighed into the night. The shite fumes were cooking up.

'Doctor who pronounced?' Hagan asked the rookie.

The rookie consulted his notebook again. 'Dr Mulligan.' He nodded in confidence at his ability to read his own handwriting now. 'Said he thinks your man died of a heart attack.'

Frank made a bullshit signalling cough.

Hagan, like Frank, knew the three doctors that currently rotated on-call to attend scenes of sudden death and perform the legally required procedure to ascertain that death has indeed occurred. Dr Mulligan is not one of them. Hagan suspected that the good Dr Mulligan was the hotel's private physician trying to earn his keep by suggesting that the cause of the man's death was natural, thereby keeping the hotel owners out of the deep shite of the Coroner's inquest possibly finding that the manner of the man's death was accidental. That finding would subsequently lead to an investigation and a further finding that the employers were negligent in their duty of care to their employees. The Coroner might then, depending on the amount of negligence, instruct the State Prosecutor to proceed with a charge of corporate manslaughter against the employers.

Hagan wrote the name of Dr Mulligan into the docketbook and put a question mark next to it. 'Your name?'

'Garda John Grimes.'

'For your records.' He peeled out one of the triplicate carbon copies from his docketbook and handed it to Garda Grimes.

Garda Grimes took it, looked at it, didn't know what to do with it, wondered if it could get him into trouble, folded it, and tucked it into his pocket.

Hagan said, 'You want to lead the way to the body then?'

Garda Grimes nodded and set off with a little less ambition.

As they passed through the narrow arteries of the service corridors that connected the vital organs of the hotel, the combined smells of bland industrial cooking and bleach wafted down the corridor, all the time getting stronger until they arrived at the kitchen where they found the white-uniformed chef's corpse lying on the floor. Standing next to the corpse was the arsed-faced detective who told them, 'I'm Detective Costigan,' and waited for the bodymen to be impressed, which they were not. His thin lips whetted with malice. 'Did you get lost?' The slippy smoothness of his oily voice reminded Frank of a Christian Brother whose every word is filled with an undercurrent of institutionalised violence. Frank had been in one of those Jesuit homes for boys, and he didn't like priests or detectives.

Hagan looked the arse-faced detective in the eyes and told him, 'It takes the time it takes,' in a tone that let the long malevolent streak of misery know that he didn't give even a tiny little fuck about what he thought.

The detective inspected his watch, breaking eye contact while making a tut-tut and sticking his chin out to establish governance over the situation. 'We'll need to get a move on.'

The bodymen ignored him and looked at the corpse, gauging the size and weight to be roughly six feet long and around eighteen stone. It was a relatively straightforward removal. First and foremost, their job is practical, requiring equal parts raw manual labour and problem-solving to ensure the removal is performed efficiently and safely with as much decorum as can be afforded under the circumstances unique to each scene of death. However, while all seemed straightforward enough, there were aspects of the presentation of the corpse Hagan knew would come up for scrutiny during the Coroner's examination. He carefully noted them. *I observed that the white coat of the deceased chef's uniform was hunched up behind the shoulders. Also, on the blue epoxy floor, there was a telltale trail through the grime from the main cooking area to the corpse, indicating that the body had been dragged across*

16

*the floor by the ankles. I also noted that the lower half of the torso showed the bluish-purple discolouration of post-mortem lividity, indicating that the body had been in place for some time.* He made his notes carefully because more than half of the cases he attends go to the Central Criminal Court as murder trials where he, being the person who took the body into the custody of the Coroner's Office, is always called upon as a witness by the State Prosecution Service who must establish a clean chain of custody for any forensic evidence that may be found on it during the post mortem examination. The bodyman, having his notes at hand in the witness box, keeps the defence council in their place while they put him under cross-examination. He is also careful to use clear handwriting as the Jury often requests a photocopy of his notes which must be then entered into evidence and distributed to the legal councils.

However, there are elements around the corpse that Hagan doesn't write into his notebook. He doesn't note that the deadman's soul has not left the scene or the strong sense of confusion and anger that hovers around the corpse like a cloud of electrical static that makes the hair stand on the back of his hands. That information he keeps to himself because there is simply no place for it in the proceedings. Society has turned death into a purely scientific procedure where all that matters is how death occurred. Death must fit into one of the four manners: natural, accidental, suicide or homicide. If Hagan were to make notes in his book about the soul of the deceased, it is safe to say that he would be laughed out of the courtroom along with the scientific portion of his notes. He would also be the first one to admit that the presence of the soul hovering over the corpse might just be his imagination. Still, even if his idea of a soul is imagined, it is equally valid to the notion that there is nothing after death since both ideas are hypotheses, and neither has any actual proof one way or the other. It is simply what he chooses to believe when he is doing his job.

The detective watched Hagan writing in his notebook and didn't like it. The notebook is a policeman's tool, used to great effect to intimidate suspects or witnesses. 'What's the notes about?'

Hagan answered him without looking up. 'The body was moved?'

Frank smiled.

The detective half nodded and cocked his nose like he'd caught a whiff of something unpleasant. 'It was. Yes…' He looked at the bodyman with as much constipated disdain as he could force onto his face.

Hagan was only a lowly bodyman, but his boss held the highest warrant in the land. 'The Coroner will want an explanation.'

The detective didn't like that, but he was a clever sléibhín with an excuse up his sleeve. 'The staff were in the middle of serving up a big banquet dinner for foreign dignitaries, heads of state, and the Taoiseach. I'm responsible for the security and safety of the whole event. I told the staff to move the body out of the way of the cookers so as no one would trip up over it, and they could get on with the work.'

The bodymen shared a look. It wasn't the first time they'd seen the inconvenient dead dragged about or put out for collection like rubbish. The one thing that all of these degraded dead had in common was that they had the misfortune to go down in their traces. There's a saying in the workplaces of Dublin: *If you dropped dead, they'd step over you.* The bodymen can attest that never a truer word was spoken.

Hagan didn't tell the detective what he thought about that. He got on with the next part of his job – tagging the body. Taking a white plastic identity bracelet from his pocket, he used a felt-tipped black pen to write the name *Marco*, followed by the letters *TBC*. Kneeling beside the corpse and carefully lifting its right hand, he made a mental note that the wrist joint was locked as he slid the bracelet onto it and fitted and fixed it there.

At the same time, Frank filled in the personal possessions docketbook, making an inventory of personal items on the body: *a yellow metal studded earring and a yellow metal necklace with a yellow metal wedding band hanging from it.* The wedding ring indicated that the dead man had a wife; maybe his body wouldn't go unclaimed after all.

The detective shifted uneasily in his squeaky leather shoes. 'We need the body out of here before the breakfast shift comes in. They can't be delayed. We've got very important people who will need a breakfast delivered on time.'

Hagan said to Frank, 'Rigor mortis has set in.' And said to the detective, 'He's been dead for more than six hours.'

The detective squirmed like something was moving quickly through his bowels. He wanted to tell this glorified van driver to go fuck himself but knew everything he said could be evidence in court. He made his excuse, for the record, 'You can tell the Coroner I decided it would be best to keep him in place until the dinner event was over and done with and the dignitaries were off to their beds. We didn't want to be taking out a body while the world press was gathered at the front doors. Did we?'

Hagan made a note of it. Carefully. 'It will be something that the Coroner will want to talk to you about,' and pointed his pen at the CCTV camera watching them from the corner. 'Make sure they don't delete the event from the camera's history.'

The detective looked at the camera, then looked at the rookie and gave him a long, thin, malicious grin.

The rookie, who was still a little high from the shite fumes, shivered and felt the chill of cold malevolence being rubbed all over him, like a human sacrifice under the giddy eye of the high priest who was going to disembowel him. It was one of those situations where the subordinate will have to take the hit to cover his superior's arse and have his young head served to the Department of Justice on a platter with a note on it making an appeal for clemency and explaining the extenuating circumstance of him being a mere postulant who didn't know any better.

Opening the fold-up stretcher, Hagan placed it next to the corpse while Frank unzipped the seven-foot-long white plastic bodybag and laid it out on the stretcher to receive the body.

The rookie asked quickly, like a child wanting to have a go, 'Can I help?

Frank, happy with the opportunity to rest his old back, stood back, 'You can take the ankles if you want.'

The rookie eagerly moved to action.

'Wait,' Hagan held up his hand. 'Do you have gloves?'

The rookie shook his head.

Frank dug into his pocket, pulled out a spare pair of latex gloves and handed them to the rookie. 'Use these.'

A snort came from the detective at the overly cautious shenanigans. 'The body's not infected with anything. It was a heart attack.'

Hagan could take the time and trouble to explain to him that we are all infected with all kinds of weird and wonderful pathogens, viruses, bacteria and fungi that are held in check by our immune system, which is constantly marshalling an army of white blood cells in a to-the-death battle against the persistent enemies, and how the balance of power changes when the body dies and stops creating new white blood cells, and the immune system's defensive legions cannot be replenished, leaving the body defenceless to be overwhelmed by the great hordes of decomposition. In this devastation, all those suppressed tribes of bacteria, fungi and parasites have their freedom day and bloom in and on the corpse. The successful ones know that their host is dead, and they change in behaviour to find a new living host. They've had millions of years of practice and have evolved with our species every step of the way, shadowing us like a hoard of predators. A roll call of the highly successful diseases that bloom on the corpse to infect a new human host would include tuberculosis, hepatitises A, B & C, HIV, cholera, E. Coli, rotavirus diarrhoea, salmonellosis, West Nile virus and typhoid. And that is why the bodymen wear gloves when they touch the dead.

Frank asked the detective, 'Have you touched the body?'

'Maybe.' The detective's mind raced through the last few hours, wherein he'd searched the dead man's pockets, found narcotics, and removed them to protect the hotel from any liability issues.

Frank saw the detective's face grow pale with worry like a wax death mask and advised him, 'Maybe you should get your bloods done to be on the safe side.'

The detective didn't have anything clever to say to that. He knew the old bodyman knew what he was talking about. You don't get to be that old and ugly by being careless.

Hagan asked the detective, 'Do we have the rest of his personal possessions?'

A perfectly blank expression fixed on the detective's face, like a non-sentient creature looking out on the world in innocent wonder.

'He didn't come to work dressed like a chef,' Hagan said and reminded the detective, 'The Coroner is a stickler for anomalies in the chain of evidence.'

The detective's nostrils flared, and his mask cracked. 'Chain of evidence? Sure, there's no crime here.'

Hagan spoke in a purposefully measured manner, 'The reason we're here is because this man has suffered a sudden death, and the manner of his death is now under investigation by the Coroner's Office. This body is in the chain of evidence of that investigation, and it is evidence that has already been tampered with. It will be for the Coroner to decide if a crime's been committed.'

'I'll check the staff locker room,' said the detective, and he walked away like he was going to find a dog to kick.

Hagan looked to the rookie, who was gloved up and twitching for action. 'You ready?'

The rookie held up his now gloved hands, delighted with himself.

'Have you lifted a corpse before?'

The rookie shook his head. 'But I lifted up an unconscious drunk last week.'

'Good start. We only need a few inches of clearance off the floor. Try to be gentle when you place the body down to avoid unnecessary post-mortem bruising.'

The rookie nodded and knotted his brow in concentration. Ready.

Frank told him, 'Take the ankles.'

When the rookie had a hold of the corpse by the ankles, Hagan took hold of it by the wrists. 'On Three. One. Two. Lift.' And that way, they moved the body off the floor and placed it into the open bodybag. It made a loud moan as it rested back into lying flat.

The rookie turned a whiter shade of pale. 'He spoke…'

Hagan assured him, 'That's just air coming out.'

The rookie was not convinced and stared at the corpse, waiting for it to say something more. 'Sounded like a word.'

'It was just air,' Old Frank said flatly and zipped the bodybag closed.

# CHAPTER THREE

2:46 A.M. The ECAS operator answered the emergency call.
'Emergency Call Answering Service. Which emergency service do you require?'

'Em … ambulance. But I think she's dead.'

'One moment. Please stay on the line.'

The operator patched the caller into the ambulance call answering division.

The caller waited.

A new voice spoke, 'Ambulance emergency. How can I help?'

'There's a girl on the ground. I think she's dead.'

'Where are you?'

'Temple Bar.'

'Where in Temple Bar?'

'Eh… think it's Bullock Lane.'

'I have your location now.' The operator told him in a reassuring voice while she typed a priority one request for an ambulance and gardai to attend to the location and began the pre-arrival procedure with the caller. 'Is she breathing?'

'Don't know.'

'Can you see if she is breathing?'

'Eh … how?'

'Put your phone on speaker. Place it near the patient, and kneel beside the patient.'

'Okay… okay. I've done that.'

'Is the patient's chest rising and falling?'

'No…'

'Put your ear close to the patient's mouth and listen. Tell me what you hear.'

After a moment, the caller replied, 'Nothing. I hear nothing.'

'Place the patient on her back. We're going to provide CPR.'

'I don't know how to do that.'

'I'm going to stay with you and talk you through it until the ambulance arrives. Okay?'

'But what if something happened to her, and I'm like, you know, touching her and getting my DNA on her and all that?'

'That won't be a concern. You'll be on record as having given first aid. Now get her on her back. Place the palm of your hand on the centre of her chest. Place your other hand on top of that hand. You have that?'

'Yes. Yes.'

'Now, with your arms straight, I want you to push down firmly, with the heels of your hands, as hard and as fast as you can. Okay?'

'Yes.'

The operator heard the effort in his voice. 'That's good. Now I want you to push fifty times - counting out loud.'

The caller began the procedure, 'One, two, three, four, five–'

'Speed it up if you can.'

'Six, seven, eight, nine–'

'That's good. You're doing great. Keep that up.'

'Fuck!'

'What is it?'

'A crack … I think I broke her ribs.'

'Don't stop. Keep going. You're doing great!'

When the caller reached fifty, his arms and shoulders were burning from the build-up of lactic acid; his lungs felt scorched, and he was out of breath and panting hard. 'I'm bolloxed!'

But the operator needed to get as many minutes of CPR out of him as she could and encouraged him back into action. 'You're doing a great job. Have a listen again.'

This break to listen was as much to allow the caller time to recover his breath as anything else.

'I hear nothing,' he told the operator.

'Okay. Let's go again. Help is on the way,' she assured him. 'Come on. Good man. Count them out to me.'

The caller began again, and the operator intervened a few times to set the pace. Each round of compressions took an average of a minute. By the fourth round, the caller's arms started to fold under the pressure of the compressions. His head spun from lack of oxygen, and his throat was dried out. 'I can't do any more... Wait. I see a Garda comin!'

2:50 a.m. Garda Sean Cummins, who was on foot patrol in the area, heard the call and made a run to the scene where he then took over giving CPR to the victim and asked the operator, 'How far out is the ambulance?'

'You should hear them soon,' the operator told him.

The caller leaned against the wall and caught his breath. 'I think I hear sirens now.'

Garda Sean Cummins was officially the first on scene.

2:55 a.m. The Dublin Fire Brigade ambulance crew arrived and took over the scene. Paramedics got to work on the young female. They quickly delivered an intraosseous infusion of adrenalin, and the resuscitation attempt continued.

Garda Cummins handed the caller back his phone. 'I'll need a quick statement from you,' he told him.

The caller nodded, got under some shelter, lit a cigarette and sucked hard on it. 'What a fuckin night.'

Garda Cummins took out his notebook, 'Can I have your name?'

'Harry Murphy.'

Garda Cummins took down Murphy's details while watching the paramedics doing their work. 'How did you find her?'

Murphy said, 'I came down into the lane to take a piss...'

Garda Cummins nodded and wrote it into his notebook.

3.15 a.m. Detective Sergeant Helen Gallagher arrived on the scene and noted the Jane Doe did not have a coat, a purse, a handbag, or ID. There were no obvious signs of injury on the body. She called in the district detective unit and the on-call doctor.

3:30 a.m.: The on-call doctor, Imelda Quinlan, pronounced death. Garda Cummins secured the scene and awaited the arrival of the district detective unit. Harry Murphy, the caller who found the body, asked Garda Cummins if he could go. Cummins requested that he wait until the detectives arrived on the scene. Harry Murphy agreed and lit another cigarette. Detective Gallagher spoke briefly with Harry Murphy and left the scene to attend to a call.

3:45 a.m. Detectives Coyle and Palmer from the District Detective Unit arrived on scene and requested the Forensic Team.

4:10 a.m. The Forensic Team arrived and examined the body of the Jane Doe and the scene. Forensic swaps were gathered from the body and the scene. They made a note of the rain and that that scene was much deteriorated and covered the body with an ambulance blanket.

4:50 a.m. The morgue ambulance was called.

# CHAPTER FOUR

'UNUSUALLY QUIET FOR a Saturday night,' Hagan says to Frank, who's half snoozing again in the shotgun seat and replies with a sceptical grunt. 'Don't count your chickens.'

He knows Frank's right. There's the usual amount of dead out there waiting to be picked up; they just haven't been found yet. But they will be found, eventually. Twenty minutes ago, they got a call for a pickup in the Temple Bar area of the City. Protocol dictates that the bodymen are never told details about the corpse for collection. The Garda calling it in would never say, "It's a suicide," because it may turn out, when the State Pathologist has completed her investigation, to be an accidental death, a natural death, or a homicide. Nobody wants to be on record as the gobshite who pronounced the manner of death on the scene. Anyway, Hagan and Frank didn't need details. They've been doing this job for over twenty years and can guess the nature of the scene they're attending by the levels of anxiety and urgency from the Call Answering Division. Sudden deaths in public places that affect the movement of goods and people have a level of urgency, as do high-profile gangland killings. Most removals, however, are performed without any fanfare: The homeless who die of hypothermia in a doorway; the suicides who find quiet places in parks, woods, garden sheds, cars parked at a favourite view, in the sea, in the river, in the lake, or their bed; the accidental falls of the elderly; the domestic homicides committed in the privacy of the home, the familicides and infanticides – all of these are collected quietly.

As Hagan makes his way quietly along the narrow streets to the location in a back lane, he has a fair idea that the body they're going to pick up is most likely an unfortunate homeless person. It's the kind of pickup that's becoming more frequent as Dublin's homeless population booms. The one snag with the location is that it's smack bang in the middle of the late-night party district of the city known as Temple Bar. As the ambulance nears the Square, the racket of the revellers rouses Frank from his snooze. 'We there?'

'Not yet.'

Frank returns to snoozing mode as Hagan turns the corner to see a great multitude dancing in the rain like happy heathens on their way to hell.

Frank opens one eye. 'Hit the sirens and lights.'

'Too crowded. Would start a stampede.'

Frank nods. 'Suppose.'

Hagan gently nudges the ambulance through the biomass that's clogging the road.

The ambulance phone rings and Frank taps it to answer. 'Dublin City Morgue. Frank Ryan speaking.'

The voice of Linda in dispatch flows out of the speakers in the dashboard like a liquid country lilt. 'Are yous lost or what, lads?'

'Nearly there now, Linda,' Frank says. 'Stuck in a crowd of headbangers – just by the Merchant's Arch.' And he bounces the ball back into her side of the court. 'If you have anyone in the area, maybe you can send someone to assist?'

'I'll give it a go for you,' she says. 'But only because it's you.'

'I'll remember you in me prayers.' He hangs up and sniffs. 'Can you smell that?'

Hagan sniffs. 'No.'

'Fuck. I can smell the smell again.'

'The smell?'

'Yeah.'

'Really?'

'Fuckssake. It's only when I wake up. Is that fuckin weird, or what?'

'It's weird. Maybe you should go to the doctor.'

'And tell him what? I smell that smell. How the fuck would he even know what I'm talking about. He would never have ever smelt the smell.'

27

'You never know.'

'Only a handful of people have smelled the smell, and you and me are two of them. Anyway. What's he going to say? Your nose is working.'

'Dunno. Like maybe it's a sign of something.'

'Sign of what?'

Hagan knows it could be a sign of changes in the brain and not good changes, but he isn't going to say that. No one likes the bearer of bad news. He throws in a stupid option. 'Some kind of sinus thing or something.'

'Some fuckin doctor you'd be.' Frank stares out into the night. He kind of knows it's not good, but he just doesn't want to go through all the bullshit. If he's learned one thing from this job, it's that there are worse things in this life than death.'

The smell Frank's referring to is the sweet stink of human decomposition created in the morgue ambulance by the countless corpses carried in it over the years. This stink is impervious to all known cleaning products and penetrates the ambulance's metal body and the bodies of those who work in it. The good news is that once the stink penetrates your body to your bone marrow, you don't smell it anymore. Your brain receptors simply stop registering the concoction of offending molecules. The downside is that people will smell it when in your presence without being able to identify it. But their subconscious will recognise it as the scent of death and activate their vagus nervous system, sending out run-for-your-fucking-life signals, making them uneasy around you. Animals smell it from you a mile away. Cats and dogs will not come near you. Budgies and other caged animals will be triggered to wreck their cells like psychotic prisoners. If you go to the zoo, you'll likely start a riot in the monkey cellblock. The only animals that tolerate the odour of a corpse are hearse horses, for they, like the undertakers, have grown accustomed to it. Of course, some creatures, like carrion eaters, live by death's unique chemical signature. It would not be unusual to discover the odd fly following you home after dealing with a ripe corpse. Frank's been doing this job for over thirty years. He shouldn't be smelling it. He opens his window a crack to let in some fresh air. The howl-singing from the various buskers competing like baying wolves and the crowd joining in form a cacophony of all the horrible noises humans can make.

Hagan says, 'It's like a sing-song at the fuckin zombie apocalypse.'

Frank laughs a little, but a vague anxiety rises in him, and his knee aches.

'Your knee at you?'

Frank rubs it. 'Hmm.'

Old Frank's knee is a kind of weathervane that warns him whenever they're on their way to pick up a child. But this didn't feel like a child to Hagan because he knows that Linda in Dispatch would have been emotional. However, something's definitely pinging Frank's knee.

'Might be just this easterly weather. Plays havoc with me rheumatism,' says Frank, forensically examining the raindrops running down the windshield like he might find some evidence there. 'Makes you wonder what's in it.'

Hagan nods. 'We still get that radioactive rain from Chernopill once or twice a year.'

'And Fuckasheema.'

'The world is bollixed.' Hagan hopes it's the radioactive rain that's fucking with Frank's knee and not a dead child. He keeps on gently nudging the ambulance through the crowd that begrudgingly yields to him, inch by reluctant inch. He understands the resentment at their presence. There's not supposed to be a morgue ambulance in the middle of their street party. The crowd look at the bodymen like they're a pair of concerned parents who've come to the party to check for drugs and spoil their fun, to remind them to be careful, to remind them that they are mortal, to remind them about death. A champion of the people emerges from the heart of the crowd, bursting with revolutionary zeal, stands in front of the ambulance like Big Jim Larkin with his hands in the air and shouts. 'You shall not pass!' Then he rummages in his zipper and takes out his penis, shakes it to life, and pisses on the headlights. A few of his mates get their penises out and start waving them about in solidarity. The girls cheer them on, and then half a dozen of them join in the protest, showing their breasts to the headlights and the cheering audience.

Hagan stops and watches the fuck-death-haka.

Frank sighs.

Hagan nods in agreement and waits…

Of the seven virtues that'd been wrought into Hagan's mortal fibre as a child by the Christian Brothers, it was patience that he excelled in. He was told more than once that he had the patience of Saint Monica, who was the Patron Saint of patience and wayward children. Perhaps she might not be so patient with the wayward children waving their cocks and flashing their tits at her. Maybe Hagan has even more patience than Saint Monica.

Frank drums his fingers on the dashboard. 'Did you ever do stuff like that when you were young?'

'Pissed out of an upstairs window in school onto the head Brother one time.'

Frank smiles. 'You didn't.'

'Fucker was smoking his pipe. Three of us did it at the same time.'

'And what happened?'

'Was our last day in the school. He couldn't do anything.'

'Love it.'

'Old fucker roared so hard that his false teeth flew out across the yard.'

Frank nodded. 'Lovely.'

'You?'

Frank shrugs. 'I was one of those gullible gobshites that thought that by behaving meself I would get me ahead in the world.'

'Didn't have you down for a good boy.'

'Never judge the book.'

A cold wave of rain arrives with force, and the penis-waving and breast-bouncing protest runs out of steam. The revolutionaries retreat from the affray with honours into the back-slapping crowd. At the same time, a large, high-visibility Garda comes into view, working her way through the crowd as if it were a herd of cattle, shouting at them, 'Yup there. Move now. Move now. Yup. Yup. Yup.'

'Advantages of growin up on a farm right there,' Hagan says.

Frank nods in agreement. 'Country people have a lovely way with animals and drunks.'

The giant Garda makes her way to the front of the ambulance, waves to Hagan and shouts, 'Come along, come along,' and walks ahead – clapping her hands and parting the sea of drunks with her magic cattle-moving word, 'Yup there. Yup there. Yup. Yup. Yup.'

Hagan gratefully moves the ambulance along behind her and imagines the kind of mincemeat she'd make of criminals who crossed her path.

'God be with the days,' says Frank as if reading his partner's mind.

Hagan nods in agreement.

A hundred yards or so along the cobblestoned road, just past the revellers, the big and beautiful high-visibility Garda stops.

Hagan lowers the window. 'Thank you. Where are we going?'

'Up along the lane there and in on your right. Kind of a side lane thing goin on in there, and you go down into it and come to a dead end.'

'Thanks again.' Hagan eases the ambulance on down the narrow laneway for fifty yards, stops and looks into the even narrower offshoot of a back lane. 'Tight.'

'You won't get a turnaround down there.'

Hagan thinks about the long walk with the gurney in the rain… 'I'll reverse in.'

Frank nods in agreement.

Hagan begins manoeuvring the rear of the ambulance into position. The reverse lights flood the curtain of rain. The rearview camera screen on the dashboard shows a ghostly grey-green picture of the narrow passage. He eases into it.

Frank watches the walls close in. 'You'll lose them mirrors…'

'Haven't lost a mirror yet.'

At the end of the laneway, skips overflowing with rubbish, piles of old office furniture and heaps of black bags filled with unknown contents are illuminated by the headlights of a Garda car and an unmarked detective's car. Amongst the rubbish, they see a red ambulance blanket that covers the corpse.

Frank goes to the back of the ambulance and gets the bodybag and gurney while Hagan goes to the body to tag it; as he comes close to it, he sees a small pale hand protruding from under the red ambulance blanket and knows in that second that the body they've come to collect is that if his daughter, Molly. He runs to her and pulls back the blanket to see her porcelain face, cradles her to him, and feels the dead weight of a corpse in his arms. He knows that no matter how hard he holds her body, no matter how loud he cries to the heavens, no matter how hard he begs God, nothing is going to

31

bring her back to life. Frank runs to him and begins saying all the things that they say when they are trying to remove the body of a dead child from the arms of a grieving parent. At the same time, the attending Gardai collectively slip their arms gently around the distraught father in unison like a loving octopus, and Molly's corpse is eased away from him.

The energy to fight leaves him.

Detective Sergeant Helen Gallagher comes to him, saying softly, 'Come on, William.'

His head spins, and a great pain consumes the entirety of his chest. In a dazed state, he's brought to a patrol car and put into the back seat. Gallagher sits beside him, holding his hand, talking softly, saying things he won't remember. Through the windscreen, he watches Frank going about his work; it seems like he is seeing death for the first time. The pain spreads to every part of him, consuming him. Then, all goes black.

He wakes suspended in a pool of blinding light. He thinks he's dead, but that thought fades as his eyes adjust on an IV bag hanging from a stainless steel pole and focus on clear liquid dripping like timed teardrops into the drip chamber. He follows the liquid's journey through the solution filter, into a long PVC tube, through the roller clamp, into the injection port and into the Luer slip connector that's connected to the cannula in his dorsal arch vein in his hand, delivering the medication that makes his body and mind numb like a sentient corpse. 'Molly.' His chest fills with pain again. A nurse with a kind face and a warm voice walks to him and explains that he's had a bit of a turn and it's important that he rests while she adjusts the dial on the roller clamp, increasing the amount of sedative entering his body. He feels his mind being pulled back into unconsciousness. He fights it, but the chemicals win. The pain leaves him. He becomes calm. All his terrible thoughts sink into the abyss, and he is pulled with them.

The next time he opens his eyes, Frank's tired face comes into view.

Frank rubs him on the other shoulder and says, 'Take it easy now.'

He grasps for the time. 'How long?'

'You've been out for a few hours.'

He closes his eyes, and when he opens them again, Frank is gone, and it's night. The room is quiet. The machines beep. Somewhere in the corridor, a nurse moves along in squeaky-soled shoes, going about her business, taking care of people. He removes the cannula from his hand and sits up. His head spins, but he holds on until it stops. He's groggy and slow. He moves carefully, thinking one solid thought at a time. His clothes are in a plastic bag at the end of the bed. He puts them on and then walks out. Nobody pays him much heed as he makes his way through the sleeping corridors.

Outside of the hospital, the cold air feels good on his face. He sets off along the empty streets. A lone taxi out on the prowl slows, looking for business, and passes on when he doesn't wave it down. As he walks, her presence comes to him, walking beside him, and he is reminded of all the mornings he walked her to school until she was big enough to go with her friends. One part of his mind tells him that her presence is a sense memory; another part tells him that it is her soul. It's up to him to choose which of the two options to believe. He chooses to believe she is with him. The grip of the pain that is set around his heart like cement eases. It takes two hours, or thereabouts, to walk home, and by the time he reaches the front door of his house, a clear question has surfaced through his foggy thoughts: what was the manner of Molly's death? The blood quickens in his head, and he fights off the dizziness that comes with the sudden surge in his blood pressure. He enters his home and knows it's empty. He takes his car keys from the bowl on the hall table. Thirty minutes later, he's at the entrance to the morgue, punching the keycode into the door. He goes to the fridge room and reads the ledger on the stainless steel table. Molly is in fridge 3B. Putting on a pair of gloves, he opens the fridge, slides the body tray out, and opens the bodybag carefully to reveal the corpse of his daughter. For some time, maybe minutes, maybe an hour, maybe more, he stands looking at her face until his mind starts to work again. He begins a procedure that he's watched the pathologist do countless times and examines her hands for defensive wounds and her nails for any breakages or evidence of a struggle. He checks her neck for bruising, but there are no signs of violence on her body.

'William?'

He turns to see the State Pathologist, Doctor Cullen, beside him. She says, 'You can't be in here now.'

He has nothing to say.

She softly takes him by the arm. 'Let me look after her now,' and leads him away from the body as Frank comes to him. 'Frank will take you home…'

On the drive home, Frank seems like a friend he hasn't seen in a lifetime. The journey is made in silence.

'Let's get you inside,' Frank says as they pull up outside of the house.

Some minutes later, Hagan is sitting at the kitchen table with a mug of strong tea in front of him, and Frank is sitting opposite. They don't talk while they drank the tea. There's no need to. These two men have been in close company for years, and they'd been around tragedy long enough to know that words don't make anything better.

Hagan asks, 'Is she for her PM today?'

'She's first on the list this morning.'

They both look at the kitchen clock.

Hagan nods. 'You have a job to do.'

Frank rinses out his mug in the sink, 'Will you call me if you need to?'

Hagan nods and asks, 'Will you let me know as soon as you know?'

'I will.' Frank goes to the door, stops, and asks, 'How's Val holding up?'

Hagan shakes his head. 'She's with her sister.'

'You shouldn't sit here on your own.'

Hagan wants to tell him that he isn't alone; Molly is with him. 'Will you tell me … if anything suspicious turns up in the PM?'

Frank nods and leaves the house.

Hagan thinks about calling Val, but the thought doesn't lead to action.

# CHAPTER FIVE

MOLLY'S BODY HAS so far been cared for by the person who found her, the first garda to attend the scene, the ambulance crew, the doctor who visited the scene and pronounced her dead, Frank, who removed her body from the scene and brought it to the morgue, the morgue technician who prepared her body for a post mortem examination, the pathologist who carried out the post mortem examination, the morgue attendant who sutured the body closed, the undertakers who collected her remains from the morgue and brought them to Mister Grogan at his funeral home where the embalmer restored the appearance of life so that friends and loved ones may view her. Now, she waits to be dressed, coffined, viewed and buried.

'Will you have a cup of tea, Father?'

'I will. Thank you, Valerie.'

The arrangements for burial begin with the priest calling to the house. And like all business conducted in Val's kitchen, it involves tea and a plate of biscuits. There is something strangely soothing about doing ordinary things in the worst of times, like attending the cabaret while the world burns. This is the time when everyone comes to the home of the bereaved when there are lots of things to organise and arrange for Molly. Even though she is no longer in the world, she is the centre of the universe for the whole community.

Hagan goes out to the back garden, to the shed, to something small and insignificant that needs to be done, something involving a tiny screw and a nut.

Valerie places the cup of tea on its matching saucer in front of the priest and apologises for her husband's behaviour. 'I'm sorry about that, Father.'

'Don't apologise to me, Valerie. Would you like to pray for Molly?'

'I would.'

She sits, and the priest begins a decade of the rosary. Each Hail Mary soothes Val's heart, and she imagines that the Mother Of God is comforting her daughter in heaven. When they're finished, the priest says, 'Let your faith be a comfort to you now, Valerie. Be certain in the fact that she is with the Lord and she is surrounded by his love.'

Valerie takes pure comfort in that.

The priest takes out his notebook, and they choose the readings and who will do them, and he goes over what he will say about Molly, about her life. He'd like to say that he gave her the first two of her Holy Sacraments of Christening and First Holy Communion. He also prepared her for her Holy Confirmation. He wants to mention how beautiful her voice was and how he always enjoyed her presence in the school choir. The singing voice for him is a gift from God and a true sign of His grace. He wants to mention what a great sorrow and privilege it is to administer her Last Sacrement and pass her into heaven. He asks Val if she has chosen someone to give the eulogy. She says she will leave that job to her husband. The priest suggests that she and her husband sit down and write the eulogy together.

Hagan dismantles the carburettor of the old Honda 50 motorbike that he refuses to give up on. He bought it brand spanking new when he was in the army and took Val out for spins on it when they started dating. He took her to places she'd never been: Skerries, Wicklow, The Sally Gap, even Wexford and Waterford. When she became pregnant, the bike rides stopped, and he got himself an old Cortina MK4 that served him well. He kept the Honda, though, in the shed, like a pet, and looked after it. He likes to take it out for a spin, up to Howth Head in the summer, sometimes when the weather is good, and sometimes even if it's raining. She doesn't have the poke for the hill climb that she once had, but she gets up there, and he has a pint in the Summit, sometimes a second pint and a bag of crisps to soak it up, and then coming back down the hill is a whole other story. She glides. She glides like a young thing again. They both do.

As he undoes the tiny screws and places them carefully on a rag, his mind works on an aspect of Molly's post-mortem examination that pulls at him: Samples of her blood have been sent for toxicology, as were swabs taken from her body. It will be some weeks before these results come back, but he knows why the swabs were taken: the pathologist found evidence of sexual intercourse. Of course, that doesn't mean rape. But he knows that Molly doesn't have a boyfriend, and he'd like to know who she had sex with on the night she died. He'd like to find him. He'd like to talk to him. He'd like to dismantle him … screw by screw. He'd also like to know the results of the toxicology. The only thing that gives him a morsel of sanity right now is the fact that the Coroner is going to investigate Molly's death. He's hanging on to that with everything he has in him.

The next piece of official business for Molly is the undertaker calling to the house. Mister Grogan would often say, privately, that funerals are not for the dead; they are for the bereaved – a rite of passage for their terrible grief. In the case the Hagan's grief, that passage is paved with flowers from the community. The front garden of the house is almost covered with them when Grogan arrives, and it is only beginning.

After the condolences and the cups of tea are put on the table, Grogan gets down to business. Over his lifetime of working with the bereaved, he's learned that the last thing loved ones want to do is to beat around the bush. Things need to be done and it's best to get straight to it. The Hagan's have lost a child who needs to be taken care of. The first thing to be decided is cremation or burial.

'We have a family plot in Glasnevin,' Val tells him.

Hagan had purchased a beautifully positioned double plot some years ago when they buried his mother, and it was already agreed between himself and Val that they would go into it. They never imagined that Molly would be going into it before them. Grogan writes the fees for opening the grave and the burial in black ink on letter-headed paper. The next decision is the church.

'Saint Joe's,' Val says, 'and Father Mick will do the ceremony.'

The fees for the church are added to the list. Grogan comes to the next piece of business, and opens out his folder that contains pictures of coffins and linings and fittings. Both Hagan and Val know what kind of coffin Molly would want, so there's no need to view the selection.

'She'd like the wicker,' Val said. And she watches Grogan write it down, and then she adds, 'Can it have a pink lining?'

Grogan nodded, 'Shade?'

'Champagne.'

Grogan asks, 'Will you want her to repose at home?'

'Absolutely. Here in the living room.' She looked around, seeing things she had to do. 'I'll get it ready for her.'

Grogan asks, 'Hearse and one family car?'

Val thinks, looks at her husband and asks him, 'What do you think?'

Hagan says, 'She loved horses.'

Val says to Grogan, 'A horse-drawn hearse.'

Grogan records it and closes his book. 'I'd imagine your friends in the choir will do the hymns?'

Val nods.

Grogan says, 'At some point, you can choose the clothes you would like Molly to repose in.'

Val asks. 'When will we have her home?'

'Tomorrow.'

Val does the sums. 'Friday morning for the funeral.'

Grogan nods.

Val closes her eyes. There's something in getting Molly home that fills her with warmth. Maybe her unconscious mind thinks all is well; Molly's coming home – it's all been a big misunderstanding.

Grogan stands, his knees creaking and cracking. He doesn't normally venture out of his funeral parlour to visit houses, but this is different. Again, the condolences are given, and Grogan makes his way to his car.

Val is motionless for a moment and looks at the ceiling. 'That lovely gown she bought for her debs….'

Hagan smiles. 'Beautiful.'

'Will you write the eulogy?'

Hagan nods. 'Do you want to do it with me?'

She shakes her head. 'Just say how wonderful she was.'

He takes some paper and a pen and goes out to the shed.

She goes upstairs to find the debs dress.

In his shed, in the night, amongst his tools and allsorts that he keeps in case he needs them, Hagan writes his eulogy for Molly, focusing on her passion for her acting and her tremendous optimism and appetite for life. There's nothing in it about her death because he doesn't want it to stain her memory. When he finishes, he sits out in the back garden looking up at the stars, unable to sleep and reluctant to be fully awake, between the worlds. In the Erebus, he finds markers, guiding facts that he follows and thinks on. The pathologist has called Molly's manner of death accidental; the mechanism of her death being a brain seizure and the cause most likely drugs, to be confirmed with toxicology reports – but there is one glaring anomaly in it for Hagan: The presence of drugs in Molly's system. He is sure that Molly wouldn't touch drugs. The sexual activity makes him think that she might have been spiked. And the presence of Detective Sergeant Helen Gallagher from the Serious and Organised Crime Unit on the scene was out of place. He's been on enough murder scenes to know that the homicide detective first looks for that which does not belong. Gallagher did not belong on the scene of an accidental drug death. It's along these thoughts that he travels from the night into the predawn and then on into the new day.

Val spends the night lying on Molly's bed, in a deep primal connection to the chemical scent of her child. The debs dress that Val's picked out for Molly's reposal hangs on the door, almost alive. Val watches it all night. At first, its green satin shimmers in the moonlight, and then it fills with the colour of the morning Sun. She sits up in the new day with purpose. There is lots to be done. The house must be made ready for Molly coming home.

At three o'clock, the neighbours come out and stand at their gates. Molly is on her way. Val and Hagan come out to the front door as the hearse turns onto the road and makes a slow procession to the house. As it passes each neighbour, they bless themselves. Mister Grogan drives the hearse, and two strong mutes sit in it with him.

Val watches it coming for as long as she can and then goes inside to sit down in the front room, which is now empty of furniture save for two chairs, one for her and one for Hagan, to keep their vigil.

As the mutes move to the back of the hearse, Hagan joins them to help carry in the coffin, and then, out of nowhere, Frank appears with some others that Hagan knows, and they carry Molly's remains into the house and place her coffin on a curtained stand in the centre of the room.

Grogan asks Val. 'Is this okay for you?'

Val thinks for a moment, then says, 'Maybe against the wall.'

Against the wall felt better to her so that people would not stand around but come in, pay their respects and move out again.

Once all is as it should be, the coffin is opened, and everyone leaves Val and Hagan to sit with their daughter. Some hours pass in silent privacy. Outside, neighbours and friends wait quietly, some saying silent decades of the rosary. Then Val makes some final touches to her daughter's hair, and when she is satisfied, the front door is opened; the viewing and paying of respects begins. They come in a procession that lasts late into the evening. Each mourner hugs Val and Hagan. Tightly. Tears flow. Sobs break involuntarily. Words are inadequate. They stand at the coffin and openly weep for the beautiful girl that's lying in it. If raw grief could bring back life into the dead, then Molly would open her eyes. Hagan watches every young man that crosses his path, trying to see if there is a tell, something to give away which one of them has been with Molly. But they are all equally emotional, and it is impossible to pick one out. However, there is one of Molly's college friends that Hagan is on the lookout for: Deirdre the student director. When he finds her, he asks her, 'Would you like to say a few words at the mass?'

Deirdre inwardly recoils from the idea. 'I don't think I would... be able.'

'That's fine,' he says. 'I understand.'

But then she rallies. 'But maybe I could. Yes.' She thinks. 'I'd be honoured.'

He smiles. 'Just a few words about who she was in college.'

Deirdre thinks about that for a moment. 'She was great craic.'

'Say that then. I don't really know what she was like, you know when she was with her friends.'

Deirdre nods, but she feels the question in there, feels that he is searching. She says, 'Everyone loved her.'

Hagan nods.

She moves closer to him. 'I wasn't with her,' she says. 'That night.'

'Of course. I understand.'

But Deirdre wants to make her point. 'The party was for that agency that she was with.' And she doesn't hide her disdain for the company that Molly was in. 'What they're saying about her is lies.'

Hagan's head takes a quick spin and recovers. 'What are they saying?'

'You haven't seen it. On Chatter?'

'What's that?'

'An app. You know, social media.'

'I don't know about… What is it that they are saying?'

'Maybe you should wait until after—'

'You can tell me now, pet.'

Deirdre takes her phone out opens the app and the post in question, and shows it to him.

Hagan reads it; his blood comes to a boil as a picture of Molly appears and the headline PARTY QUEEN DRUG DEATH.

He gathers himself. 'Who… Who posted that?'

Deirdre shrugs. 'Who knows?'

'I don't follow…'

'It's anonymous.'

Hagan makes a mental note of the name of the app and calms himself. 'Thank you, Deirdre.' Before he lets her go, he asks her, 'Did Molly have a boyfriend?'

Deirdre takes a moment before she answers and says very definitely, 'No.'

'You're sure?'

'I'm positive.'

Hagan examines that. How can she be so positive?

Deirdre adds, 'Molly wasn't into boys.'

She waits for the penny to drop, and when it does, she hugs him and says in his ear, 'She was the most beautiful person I ever met,' and she walks away from him.

The house empties by ten o'clock. They both sit with Molly for the rest of the night, keeping their parental vigil. Val hasn't heard any of the online gossip, and Hagan will not be the one to tell her about it. But he wonders why someone would go out of their way to blacken Molly's name. This was another clue that something was not right about her death.

'I won't be able to be here after…' Val says.

Hagan comes out of his thoughts. 'What's that?'

41

'After we bury our daughter. I won't be coming back into the house.'

He thinks about that.

She doesn't say any more about it.

After an hour, maybe it's more, he says, 'Where will you…'

'Anne.'

'In Spain?'

She nods.

'For how long?'

'I have no idea.'

It's good that she is going to Spain. He's going to be busy here. He has people to find and things to do to them.

# CHAPTER SIX

THE PHONE BUZZES on his bedside locker like a carrion fly in a death spasm; he grabs it and taps the glowing screen. 'Coroner's office. William Hagan speaking.'

A warm voice with a soft country lilt fills the darkness. 'Morning, William. What's the craic?'

'All good, Linda. How're things with yourself?' His back delivers a warning stab of pain as he peels himself out of the bed.

'Could be better. But hey, who's goin to listen to me grumble? Huh? Am I right?'

'You are.' He wraps an elasticated rubber back brace around his girth and pulls it tight like he's saddling up a horse. 'What've you got for me?'

'Sending the address now.'

Support brace in place, he puts on his blue uniform trousers that hang on the back of the chair. The phone pings with the location of a corpse for collection. 'Got it.' He puts on his blue shirt and receives a second stab of pain between the L1 and L5 discs of his lumbar region that twists with a vengeance and torments him while he bends to put his socks on. 'Has the deceased been pronounced?'

'Definitely.'

Carefully, he straightens up, allowing the nerve pinched by a worn-out disk to ease into a less painful place. 'Okay. Got it. On the way.'

'The on-scene Garda asked for a silent approach into the estate. Says it can be a bit volatile around there. They don't want to wake them all up.'

'Silent approach it is. Thanks, Linda.' He points his finger at the glowing red button on the screen.

'Be careful,' she says. 'The roads are shite.'

The malevolent stew of pain being cooked up in his lower back starts to bubble up his spine. He needs some chemical intervention before it reaches his head.

'I better get rolling. Thanks, Linda.'

'How are you holding up?' Her voice is infused with concern.

Usually, anybody on the graveyard shift is always in the humour for a chat. The darkness makes the world a lonely place. The nocturnal sentinels keeping a vigilant watch over the sleeping city stick together. He used to be up for the chat, but not anymore. 'All's good, thanks, Linda. Better get a move on,' he says, quickly tapping the red button on the screen to end the conversation before she can hook him with another question. His aggravated spinal nerves sing in painful harmony, encouraging his legs and arms to join in the crippling chorus as he makes his way out of the bedroom and along the upstairs landing, where he pauses at the door to Molly's bedroom. She's in there peacefully sleeping. He's sure of it. He moves on carefully so as not to wake her, making his way downstairs to the kitchen. He likes moving about the house in the night. It comforts him. He feels her presence more when it is like this, a communal space between their divided worlds.

By the time he gets to the kitchen tap, the pain is attacking him with growing strength, shooting down his legs and threatening to take them hostage from under him. But no matter what kind of pain comes from his abused body, it's nothing that a few weapons-grade painkillers won't rub out. Taking a foil card from his pocket, he presses the plastic blisters and pops out two white pellets with a satisfying click, puts them into his mouth, chews and swallows them with a mouthful of cold water. The payload of opioids rushes through his bloodstream and hits the pain receptors in his brain, forming barricades and securing the realm of the mind. He will soon be comfortably numb, and governance will be restored over the unwilling flesh.

Hail crashes in waves on the kitchen window, but the new triple-glazing mutes it and makes it seem like he's watching the storm on a television screen with the sound turned down. He likes this violent northeast weather that comes into Dublin Bay sideways on the city's northern flanks. If you're caught out in it unprepared, you're fucked. He's always prepared. The grip of pain on his spine is suddenly released. He exhales deeply into the beautiful absence. Time to move on.

Navigating the hallway, he steps over Molly's shoes scattered around the floor, having been kicked from her feet in protest at the injustice of her mother's *no-shoes-in-the-house* rule. Val would not pick them up after her. And so the shoes would sit at an impasse, a fault line in the mother-daughter relationship. So, like an undercover peacekeeper, he'd clandestinely pick up the offending articles and place them in the cabinet. Both sides of the standoff would think the other party had given way – life would move on. But now, these scattered shoes will stay where they are – preserved in place like the historical artefacts of a lost civilisation.

Stepping into the small porch at the front door, he puts on his working boots that never cross the threshold of his home because of the places they have been. As he bends to lace them up, there's no activity from his back – the miraculous army of opioids has taken complete control of the region now.

He senses her presence.

A soft, sleepy voice speaks from behind him, 'I'll make you some breakfast, Dad.'

He doesn't look around. 'It's four in the morning, Darling.' Sometimes, if he looks, she vanishes.

'Is it?'

In his peripheral vision, he sees her standing on the stairs in her nightdress, the long yellow cotton one that makes her look like a pilgrim, rubbing her eyes and blinking them open wide, then squinting into the darkness. 'Dad, you're not going out in that weather, are you?' She walks down the stairs and joins him in the porch, her pale bare feet oblivious to the cold tiles. He dare not move. She holds her mop of red curls out of her face with one hand and examines the night like it's the first time she's seen it. 'Weird. It looks like somewhere else out there.'

'Somewhere else?'

'When you see it like this. It's like it's somewhere else. Isn't it?'

He looks out at the cul-de-sac of twelve redbrick houses huddled together in a circle like one of the ancient raths that once covered the land around here to fend off pillaging Norsemen who came in with

45

this northeastern front. Maybe their souls are still raiding in the storm. Maybe Celt souls are once more standing out in the elements to defend their land. Maybe storms are made of ancient battling souls.

He asks, 'Are you cold?'

'No.' She smiles. 'Did you get a cup of tea, even?'

'I'm fine, Pet.' Without thinking, he moves out of years of habit and kisses her on the forehead. She vanishes. He waits and looks again and sees her on the stairs.

She yawns, 'Love you, Dad.'

'Love you too, sweetie. Go back to bed.'

She turns and heads back up the stairs.

He watches her go and waits, but he has no idea what he's waiting for...

The carriage clock on the mantlepiece in the living room ticks loudly, chopping time into bite-sized pieces and reminding him that a corpse is waiting to be collected. He remembers his purpose and slides his arms into his long black rubber raincoat, buttons it, pulls up the high collar and steps out of the porch to be punched in the face by a fistful of hail like the storm was just waiting for him to come out so it could batter him. He pushes his way through it to the morgue ambulance parked in his driveway, the hail slapping his cheeks fast in a left-right combo like it's putting manners on him, but all the time, his head is filled with the warm glow of chemically induced wellbeing.

Reaching the ambulance, he jumps in and quickly closes the door behind him, sealing himself in the safe cocoon of the cab, enjoying the surge of burning heat on his slapped face. When he was young, people said he had a face only a mother could love because the contours of his jawline looked too big. He was generally big-boned and awkward, but through the years of ugly adolescence, he grew into those big bones, and his big jaws transformed into the face of a handsome man. But his formative years of being ugly stayed with him so that he never leaned into his good looks, never slipped into vanity. He prided himself on being a plain and ordinary man.

Peeling out of his overcoat and putting it on a hook behind him, he turns the ignition key to deliver a twelve-volt jolt of life-giving electricity that shocks the engine into life. The four pistons lurch in turn to explode small amounts of diesel fuel in the cylinders and create the energy to turn the crank while simultaneously sucking in more of the explosive mixture. The engine makes a series of aggravated coughs like an old forty-a-day smoker before getting the necessary fluids and oxygen ratio into the system to form continuous internal combustion. The spluttering eases away and settles into a steady rhythm. The dashboard lights up with red icons warning him to hold his horses and wait a minute. He waits the required minute until the engine sorts itself out. The red warning signs turn off. The engine's vital systems are green and good to go. He's good to go, too. Man and machine are in harmony.

With the defog blower on fast and the wipers on slow, the windscreen clears as he eases the vehicle carefully out of the driveway and then forward along the black tar road out of the sleeping enclave. Here and there, a bedroom light is burning, and streetlights show cross-section samples of the weather's anatomy. There's not a creature out in it. He turns onto the main road, flicks on the emergency lights and floors the accelerator. The engine growls as it's fed plenty of juice, and the pistons rapidly increase their revolutions by thousands per minute. The crankshaft transfers all that power to the drive wheels, and they turn faster and faster. He feels the satisfying surge of acceleration. The tyres expel the standing water into a great cloud of spray that rises like a cloak in his rearview mirrors. The rolling emergency lights fill the mist with a glittering aurora so that the flashing morgue ambulance looks like a Valkyrie chariot streaking across the night sky to collect the souls of battle-fallen Norse warriors and speed them to Valhalla.

The drugs work.

# CHAPTER SEVEN

BIG JOE RYAN sleeps like a baby in his armchair, fully dressed in his new blue polyester uniform, his sweet dreams undisturbed by the loud racket of the ringing phone.

His mother runs into the room, grabs the phone and answers, 'He's ready!'

Hagan says, 'Have him at the front door in ten minutes.'

Ten minutes later, Joe's large frame fills the doorway of his mother's small house as he waits with a cup-flask in each hand. Ready now. As the morgue ambulance arrives at the gate, he takes off in a lolloping broken trot like a plough horse that's never been out of its yoke, clip-clopping through the puddles on the path, and clambers into the passenger seat. At the same time, his mother watches from her front bay window, backlit by the stand-up lamp and dressed in her Holy Mary blue nightdress, a cigarette hanging from the side of her mouth like a worn-out mother saint in her shrine, waving to her son like he's going off to war.

Joe waves back to her and says to Hagan, 'Sorry about that. She always makes a show of me.'

Hagan drives the ambulance away. 'She loves you.'

Joe hands him one of the flasks. 'Tea. Black... I saw you makin your tea yesterday. Took note.'

'Thank you.'

'Me Ma made it.'

'Well, say thank you to your Ma for me.'

'I will.'

'Buckle up.'

Joe finds the safety belt and pulls it across his large frame. 'Is it a murder?'

'No idea.'

'Do they not tell you what it is?'

'I know it's a dead body.'

'Right. But it would be nice to be prepared.'

'We are prepared … for anything.'

Joe rolls that fact around for a bit, thinking of the endless possibilities. 'Right ... Might be a shooting?'

'Why do you think it might be a shooting?' Hagan already regrets asking.

'Me and me ma were on Gangsta Rap and — It's a chat group for —'

'I know what it is.'

'Right. Well, they're saying that someone ratted on a big drug shipment for the Delaney gang and someone's head is going for the chop.'

'Right. And eh, what do you chat about on Gangsta Rap?'

'I don't chat. I just read stuff.'

'Right… And what about your Ma?'

'She makes the odd comment to give-out about something. She had a right go at Danny Boy Delaney the other day.'

'Yeah?'

'Yeah. He's –'

'I know who he is. D'you not think that's a bit dangerous?'

'We don't use our real names. We use nicknames.'

'I have to ask, what's your nickname?'

'Kid Blast.'

'That's very cryptic…'

'And me Ma is Ma Baker Three …

'Ma Baker one and two was already taken then?'

'Yeah. They're in the choir with me Ma.'

The rain makes a constant drumroll on the ambulance's metal skin as they make their approach through the downpour, sweeping back and forth across the road in waves and gently rocking the ambulance from side to side.

Joe watches the red needle climb the face of the speedometer. 'Doesn't feel like we're doing one twenty. Very smooth.'

'That's the Mercedes for you, proper chassis and engine.'

'How fast can it go?'

'No idea.'

'How can you not know?'

'I've never pushed it that hard.'

'Not even in an emergency?'

'They'll still be dead when we get there.'

Joe contemplates that truth for a moment and comes to a bigger thought. 'Speed is all relative, really, isn't it?'

Hagan nods to indicate that he hears what Joe is saying but is not listening.

Joe goes on, 'Like, we're already spinning at a thousand miles an hour in a solar system that's travelling at four hundred and fifty thousand miles an hour around the Milky Way.

Hagan nods again with less enthusiasm.

Joe, undeterred, goes on, 'And our galaxy is travelling at one point three million miles an hour on a collision course with the Andromeda Galaxy and —'

Hagan holds up his hand. 'Get your notebook out.'

Joe gets pen and paper at the ready.

'New Rule. You ready?'

Joe nods.

'No talking in the morning.'

'Right.' Joe writes. "Not talking...'

'It's nice to be quiet in the morning.'

Joe writes. 'Nice to be quiet...'

As they near the turn off the main road to the housing estate where the corpse is waiting, Hagan says, 'You remember everything that I showed you in the morgue?'

'Yeah...'

'Good.'

'But keep on telling me what to do when we get to the scene. In case I forget.'

'Fair enough.'

Navigating the ambulance along thin roads with no working streetlights that might interfere with the nocturnal drug dealing business, Hagan sees, somewhere in the middle of the vast housing estate, a blue strobe ball of light bouncing around under the low black cloud canopy, like a party balloon trapped in a crashed car. It guides him to the crime scene that's in a tight square of redbrick terraced houses. There's no need to worry about waking the neighbours because they're up and out in their pyjamas and overcoats, smoking, drinking tea, coffee, or cuppa soups and formed in close ranks under a testudo of multicoloured umbrellas, small fold-up ones, golf-sized ones, huge ones emblazoned with the logos for various brands of alcohol that are booty from pillaged beer gardens.

Joe wipes the condensation from his passenger window with the sleeve and eyes the scene. 'Little kids and all are out.'
'What kid is going to sleep through all of this?'

As they come into the centre of the tight square of houses, Joe realises that all eyes are on the morgue ambulance. He becomes fearful and begins to breathe heavily.
Hagan picks up on the nervous change in his rookie as he eases the ambulance into a space between two Garda cars. 'Don't mind the crowd or anyone in it. Keep your eyes down and your head in the game.'
A clammy sweat suddenly covers Joe's body. 'I'm forgetting everything…'
'What?'
'Everything. I'm just forgetting it. Like me Nana when she got the memory loss thing for old people. She would just do a wee on the floor and meow like a cat.' His head feels fat and heavy, and his face goes waxy like a corpse. 'I don't… She didn't even know me name. Nothing. She just kept meowing at me.'
Hagan places a steady hand on Joe's arm. 'Listen to me. Listen … are you listening?'
'Yeah.'
'You're just having a panic attack. Have you had one before?'
'Maybe. I don't know. I think so. Probably. Yeah. All the time when I was a kid.'
'Do you take medication for it?'
'No. Should I? Maybe I should get some. Maybe I–'
'Listen. Stop thinking about all the crap.'
'I can't.'
'You can. You just need to think about the next thing you're goin to do. What is it?'
'I don't know.'

'Take a breath.'

Joe takes a conscious breath and feels the grip of the panic release a little. 'Get out? I need to get out.'

'Good. In through the nose. What d'you have to do to get out?'

Joe thinks hard. His breathing hurts like someone is poking him really hard in the chest, but he keeps at it, getting control in small bite sizes. 'Open the door.'

'Yes. Remember to breathe out. Then what d'you do?'

Joe finds the gold seam of action and follows the shining path of purpose out of the panic. 'Go to the back of the ambulance and open the back doors and get the gurney...'

'Okay. That's all you need for now. Out you get.'

Joe puts his hand on the door handle and feels the pain in his lungs ease off. 'I feel a bit better.'

'There you go,' says Hagan. 'You do the gurney. I'll do the paperwork. Don't forget the bodybag. Yeah. One thing at a time. Right?'

'Right. Gurney. Bodybag. Got it.'

'Don't forget your gloves.'

Joe welcomes the cold rain on his face as he walks to the back of the ambulance, and he starts to feel better.

Hagan pulls up his collar and puts on a pair of black latex gloves as he walks to the Garda on point duty at the garden gate. 'What are we looking at?'

The Garda says, 'Suicide. Teenager. Male.'

'Messy?'

'Hanged.'

'Upstairs or downstairs?'

'Up. Back bedroom.'

Hagan looks back to Joe, who's taking the gurney out of the ambulance. 'Leave the gurney. Get the fold-up stretcher.'

Joe grabs the fold-up stretcher and a bodybag from the back of the ambulance, being busy, sorting himself out. He proceeds, head bowed and focused on the job, one step at a time, to the house.

# CHAPTER EIGHT

HAGAN ENTERS THE narrow hallway, its walls lovingly cluttered with pictures of a handsome boy's life from birth through baby birthdays, boyhood, First Holy Communion, Holy Confirmation and teenager. Detective Sergeant Helen Gallagher of the Organised Crime Unit walks towards him with the confident swagger of a judo blackbelt. 'William, how are you?' She has a directness that makes everything she says sound like an interrogation, like no matter what answer you give her will not be believed.

'Fine. Thanks.' Hagan is not keen on her. He doesn't trust her. He wonders why she's here. It's teenage suicide. She's a detective with the serious and organised crime unit. He's been poking around the files trying to find out why she was at Molly's scene of death, but because most of the files are with the Coroner, he hasn't had much success. However, the Coroner's investigation is coming to its conclusion, and he will have access to all the files and, hopefully, the truth. Maybe Gallagher knows he's suspicious. Maybe that's why she's here. He moves the conversation to the business at hand. 'Do we have a name?'

'Rory Keegan.' She keeps on reading him, looking for a tell.

He writes the name into the docketbook, then looks past Gallagher into the kitchen, where he sees the grieving mother watching him from the kitchen door. She's in her early thirties. Pale and devastated. She makes eye contact with him. He gives her a sympathetic nod of recognition and says privately to Gallagher, 'Make sure that the kitchen door is closed when we bring him down. She doesn't need to see him in a bodybag.'

Gallagher nods and looks at Joe standing in the doorway, looking lost and curious like a creature of the forest. 'He is okay?'

'First night,' Hagan tells her.

She nods. 'He looks a bit, you know?' She taps her head.

Hagan asks her, 'Are any of us right in the head to be doing this for a living?'

She smiles. 'What's that saying? You don't have to be mad to do this job, but it helps.' Then she adds, as if she has read his mind, 'I was in the area.'

He nods and makes his way upstairs. Joe follows him to the small, tight landing that has three closed doors. A chemical concoction of spicy deodorant and flowery perfume hangs in the air. Stuck on the back-bedroom door is a yellow post-it note with very careful handwriting on it that reads: *Don't come in. Sorry Ma.*

Joe reads it…

Hagan says, 'Never mind that. We have problems to solve here. This landing is very tight. Open the stretcher out on the floor there and follow me in. Where's your gloves?'

'In me pocket.'

'Where should they be?'

'On me hands.'

'Put them on now and make sure to give your hands a good scrub when we get back to the morgue.'

'Sorry.' Joe fumbles in his pocket to get the gloves that he should have had on his hands before touching anything.

Hagan carefully pushes open the bedroom door and enters the small room to find the naked pallor mortis white corpse of a teenage male on the floor. Defibrillator pads are still in place on the chest, as is the needle used to administer an intraosseous infusion of adrenalin into the marrow of the shinbone. Scattered about the floor like leaves are various wrappings of paper and plastic that once held items of medical equipment used by fast-moving emergency workers in their effort to resuscitate a life that was ultimately too far gone to bring back into the world. The childish swollen face is oedema blue with wide open red shot eyes, and a mouth is full of engorged purple tongue that protrudes rudely at the world in a portrait of strangulation.

Hagan feels the boy is still present and distraught.

Joe is attempting to accomplish the task of opening out the fold-up stretcher that's resisting his best efforts.

Hagan resists the urge to give his rookie advice. It's important to let him figure it out. This is on-the-job training, and no two jobs are the same. When Joe finally locks the joints of the stretcher in place, he proudly puts it on the floor; job done.

'Other way,' Hagan says.

Joe looks at him.

'Flip it over. Open the straps.'

Joe flips it. Opens the straps.

What Hagan likes about his rookie is that he is teachable. You're never going to know everything in this job; all you can really hope to achieve is to learn how to think, to figure stuff out, to get the job done. The trick to problem-solving is to keep the ego out of the equation. Hagan had tried two other rookies since Old Frank retired, but neither of them lasted a week, even though both of them had worked as undertakers. One fella had himself convinced that he knew it all and had a few things to teach Hagan and then walked off the job on train tracks when they were collecting body parts. The other fella just couldn't stop puking every time they picked up a putrified corpse. Puking on crime scenes is a deal breaker. But Joe, even though it's very early days, might just be the fella for the job.

'Bring the bodybag in with you.'

Joe enters. Hagan closes the bedroom door. A sanctuary is formed. 'Okay. You see what he did?'

Joe looks at the body. Lost.

Hagan points to a bathrobe cord on the floor. 'He tied that around his neck, then put a knot in the other end, then put it over the top of the door, then closed it, jammed it there, then hanged himself with his weight.'

Joe is at a loss. 'This is a lovely bedroom. Why would he...?'

Hagan holds his hand up. 'Our only concern here is noting how we found the remains and removing them safely to the morgue.' He hands Joe the morgue docketbook and takes a white plastic morgue ID bracelet from his pocket. 'Read out the name to me.'

Joe reads from the docket, 'Rory Keegan.'

'Spell it.'

Joe spells it out.

Kneeling beside the body, Hagan fills the name into the bracelet, 'Always double check everything,' and lifts the left wrist to fasten the bracelet on it. The skin is soft, and the joint is compliant. 'We get any part of that name wrong, there will be a lot of pain and discomfort coming our way from on high. Remember that...' He sees Joe is scanning the room, wide-eyed. 'Earth calling Joe?'

'Sorry ... Chelsea posters... my team as well.'

'You don't need to get to know him. You're going to fuck yourself up, and you won't last a week if you keep that up. Do you hear me?'

'Yeah. Sorry.'

'Every single corpse we pick up has a sad story to tell. You can't tune into it all. It'll swallow you up. D'you understand me?'

'Sorry.'

'Look. The thing you have to remember here is that we're helping him. You understand that. Right?'

'Yeah.'

'And the best way to help him is by being professional, by doing your job to the best of your ability.'

'Yeah.'

'Head in the game. Open out that bodybag on the floor.'

Joe spreads and unzips the pristine white bag. The long ripping zipper sound goes through him, through the room, through the whole fucking house. He feels he's invading the deepest privacy of this boy. It's suddenly absurd to him. What the fucking hell is he doing in the boy's bedroom, taking his body away from his mother, who's crying downstairs in the kitchen? He doesn't even know who this dead boy is, and he feels suddenly intimate with him.
Hagan points to the feet of the corpse. 'Take the ankles and remember – gently. We don't want any unnecessary post-mortem bruising.'

'Right.' Joe slowly grips the ankles and then lets go of them – fast. 'He's warm.'

Hagan waits...

Joe gets a grip of himself. 'Sorry. I wasn't expecting him to be warm.'

'That's okay.' Hagan steers him back on track, 'The ankles.'

Joe grips the ankles again. The heat from the body penetrates his hands and then radiates into his arms and passes through him like a soft electrical current, like the last of the boy's life force is leaving his corpse. 'It's like he's here.'

'Of course, he's here,' Hagan says.

Joe looks worried.

'Where else is he going to be?'

Joe looks around.

Hagan says, 'You ready, on the count of three – one – two – lift' They gently lift and slide the corpse onto the open bodybag. Hagan sees a phone on the floor. The screen lights up with messages that can't be fully read, but he can see enough to know that they're threats. He places the phone into an evidence bag and then into the bodybag. 'What's on the body travels with it to the morgue. We're responsible for the chain of evidence now.'

Joe nods and considers the phrase *chain of evidence* and what it might mean, where that chain starts and ends, and what link in it he is.

Hagan points to the bathrobe cord on the floor. 'And the ligature.'

Joe puts it in the bodybag. It's evidence. It's important. He feels he is a small part of something really big, a cog in the machine of justice.

Hagan nods. 'And zip him up.'

'Me?'

'Yes. You.'

Joe feels tricked, like when his mother told him that the needle from the nurse wouldn't hurt him, and then it hurt a lot, and now he has a phobia about needles and nurses. He kneels to zip up the bag and looks at the wide red eyes that remind him of those suffering Jesus oil paintings he saw in the gallery when his nana was dying. 'Will I close his eyes for him?'

'Why would you do that?'

'Seen it on the telly.'

'Never mind what you seen on the telly. Zip him up as he is.'

Joe performs the duty of zipping up the dead boy in the bag. He's reminded of his nana zipping up his coat in the cold morning before he went off to school and secretly slipping some money into his pocket so he could buy sweeties that he wasn't allowed to have because he was too fat. She looked after him most of the time because his ma worked in the sweet factory. However, she never brought home any sweets, but she always smelled of bulls-eyes, sour-apples, fizz-bombs and other exotic concoctions that he could not identify by their smell but were the stuff of his dreams.

The bodymen men carry the bagged corpse out of the bedroom into the hall and place it on the stretcher. There's not much weight in it, but that can be deceptive and lure the corpse carrier into a false sense of security. A body in pallor mortis is as fluid as a bag of water. The weight shifts quickly in every direction, as Hagan learned many years ago at the cost of his long-suffering back.

They begin the procedure of the removal, a job of practical manual labour under the decorum of ancient ritual, taking the remains out of the house feet first. As they stretcher the corpse down the stairs, the sound of crying grows louder in the kitchen, but thankfully, the kitchen door is closed.

Hagan reads Joe. 'Don't tune into that. You hear me? That's her grief, not yours. Yeah?'
'Yeah.'

Outside of the house, all of the chatter in the square stops abruptly as the bodymen emerge with the stretchered corpse. The older neighbours make the sign of the cross and mouth silent prayers. The teenagers look on, secretly fearful. The children are wide-eyed. The only sound now is the howl of a mother's grief. The rain stops. The night listens. Hagan and his rookie secure the corpse into the back of the ambulance and remove it to the morgue.


'That's a dangerous game you're playing.' Joe watches Hagan dip a gingersnap in his tea and keep it there like he's drowning it.

'It's all under control.' Hagan waits for a second longer … then moves the sufficiently soaked biscuit from the tea to his mouth in one fluid movement and consumes it whole.

Joe is impressed. 'You must have nerves of steel. I wouldn't chance leaving it in that long.'

Hagan smiles. 'Life on the edge.'

'Have you ever tried to dip a Kitkat?'

'That's a kind of an abomination.'

'I saw a thing on youtube where someone deep-fried a Kitkat in batter.'

Hagan shakes his head. 'That youtube has a lot to answer for.' His phone rings. He answers, 'Dublin City Morgue, Hagan speaking.'

Joe waits, reading Hagan's face like an alert gun-dog.

Hagan says to the phone, 'No worries. I'll look after it.' He hangs up. 'Rory Keegan's mother is on the way in to make the ID.'

'Did she not do the ID at the house before we collected him?'

'She never laid eyes on his corpse.'

'How?' asks Joe. 'I mean, she musta seen him when she opened the bedroom door – right?'

'She didn't find him. She went upstairs and saw the post-it note on the door but couldn't open it because he'd jammed it shut with the bathrobe cord. So she ran out of the house screaming for help and got the next-door neighbour. The neighbour ran up and, got the door open, and found him. But he wouldn't let her see the youngfella like that.'

Joe nods. 'I get that.'

Hagan rinses out his mug under the tap. 'So no formal identification was made.' He hangs it on the mug tree. 'Let's make him presentable for her.'

Joe quickly tidies up his portion of biscuit crumbs and follows Hagan.

'Gloves,' says Hagan as they enter the fridge room.

Joe goes to the sink and emergency eyewash station. To the right of it is the wall-mounted first aid kit, defibrillator, and hand sanitiser. Then, a shelf that contains a box of masks, a box of identity bracelets, a box of fridge magnets, a box of sanitation wipes and three boxes of latex gloves in large, medium and small. He takes out two pairs of large gloves and hands one pair to Hagan.

Hagan says, 'There's a closet next to the viewing room – inside of it is a load of clean white sheets in a box with the word shrouds written on it. Get me two of them.'

Joe goes.

Hagan retrieves the corpse of Rory Keegan and transfers it onto a gurney, unzipping the bodybag to reveal the corpse that now bears the scars of the post-mortem examination. With a sanitised wipe, he carefully cleans the blood spatter from the face. The post-mortem procedure, which involved the removal and replacement of all of the body's internal organs, drained the blood and other fluids from the body, thereby clearing the blue of the petechiae from the face, reducing the engorged tongue and turning the skin to a sterile white. A block is placed under the head to prevent the jaws from dropping and locking the mouth wide open. The v-neck cut from shoulder to shoulder is kept below the neckline when making incisions so that the body can be viewed. Expert hands have carefully and neatly sewed the incision that runs the length of the torso. The face and hands are made clean. The eyelids have been closed. When Hagan is finished cleaning the corpse, it looks like a study in marble of a sleeping boy.

Joe arrives in with two white sheets and looks at the corpse. 'He looks different.'

Hagan nods and spreads the first sheet over the body, covering it from feet to shoulders. The second sheet is folded to make a pillow and is gently slipped between the block and the head. 'Be very careful with the head. Sometimes, there will still be fluid coming from the scars.'

Joe can't see any scars. 'What scars?'

Hagan carefully parts the hair behind the ear to reveal an incision that has been sewn closed. 'The cut goes behind the head from one ear to the next.'

Joe nods. 'What's that for then?'

'So that the scalp can be peeled forward over the face to expose the skull. Then, the top of the skull is sawed off, and the brain is removed for examination. Then it's all put back and closed up.'

Joe thinks about all of that.

Hagan moves to the desk. 'I'll get you in there at some point so you can see a full post-mortem.

Joe doesn't want to go in there, but he keeps his mouth shut.

From the desk drawer, Hagan retrieves a stainless steel comb, wets it under the tap and uses it to part the boy's hair over the post-mortem scars and settle the fringe down over his forehead. He stands back and looks at their work. 'What d'you think?'

Joe nods. 'He looks great.'

Hagan wheels the shrouded body from the fridge-room to the viewing-room.

Julie Keegan waits in the family room with a young uniformed garda. When Hagan comes in, she immediately recognises him as the man who came into her home and took her son's body away.

People think that it helps the bereaved to pour out your condolences on them, to display grief for them, like an offering of pain. But he knows the opposite is true.

'Julie Keegan?'

She nods.

He holds the door open. 'This way, please.'

Julie rises. The garda rises with her. Hagan leads the way. They follow him along the pristine rubber-floored corridor that squeaks under the soles of their shoes like they're hurting it a little bit. The smell of the building, for those who are not acclimatised to it by work, causes unease. The concoction of various odours cannot be identified. But somewhere in the air, the human senses can detect the precise chemical signature that alerts the primitive parts of the brain to death. Julie's vagus nervous system goes into overdrive, telling her body to run. But she cannot run. She is here to claim the body of her child.

They enter the viewing room and look at a pale green wall with a pale green curtain on it. This young mother is in the middle of the worst time of her life, and the cause of her nightmare is behind the curtain. A ridiculous random hope enters her mind, like an optimistic moth flying to the moon. She thinks *maybe it's not Rory*.

But the hope burns away as quickly as it came.

Time has stopped. She might have been standing in front of this curtain for hours, unmoving, maybe even for years … waiting. Maybe some part of her has always been waiting since her boy was born to open this curtain. She looks at Hagan. Did he speak to her? She's not sure. Maybe he asked her a question. She hasn't slept, and her mind is switching on and off like a lightbulb that's on the blink, flicking in and out of reality. She keeps thinking that she sees her son from the corner of her eye. Senses him near her. That's how it is at the beginning.

Hagan says, 'If at any time you feel that you cannot continue, just tell me.'

Julie nods. His voice sounds like it's coming from another room like she's outside watching herself standing at the curtain. She wants to say she can't continue before he pulls it open and removes any doubt, but she can't say that. She wants to ask, can we just go back to when I had my boy?

Hagan waits.

She nods.

He carefully pulls the chord that draws the curtains open on the window to reveal Rory's shrouded body. His face is clean and pale. He never looked that peaceful in his life, she thinks. She hopes that whatever torment drove him out of this world has not followed him into the next. There were no signs that he would do it. Or maybe, she thinks, the signs were everywhere, and she didn't see them. Every week, she'd hear about some kid taking their own life somewhere. It seemed like some kind of virus that was going around. Only a fortnight ago, she attended the funeral of one of his friends. It was like a birthday party. A carnival. But not a wake or celebration of the dead boy's life. How could it be? He was only seventeen. He didn't have a life to celebrate. So what was the celebration about? There won't be any celebrations around her son's corpse. None.

She is lost now. No longer present. She can't be. Her legs go from under her, and she leans on Hagan. She cries out in pain. Bad pain. She pours out her grief onto him. He makes no attempt to stop her. He knows where she is. A place that no parent should be. A place that he is in because he doesn't want to leave it – it is the place where Molly is. He will stay in it with her forever.

He waits.

When the cascade of grief has eased to a steady flood, he feels her getting her feet under her again and taking her weight from his shoulder. She looks into his eyes, grips his hand like a child, and asks, 'What happened to him?'

She squeezes his fingers hard so that he will give her the answer.

The question might seem absurd, given the circumstances. The boy hanged himself. But Hagan understands what she means by the question. She doesn't expect an answer. She eases her grip on him and looks to the floor.

Hagan looks to the young garda.

She's just about holding it together, but she has a job to do here. She says to Julie, 'It is required by law that I ask you, is this your son, Rory?'

All three of them look at the boy in the shroud.

Of course, there is no doubt that this corpse is that of Julie's son, but the written record cannot read that Julie cried so much that it became obvious that that dead boy was her son. Verbal identification must be made. If the next of kin is not up to viewing the body, identification can be made through DNA. They wait.

Julie's eyes stay fixed on her dead boy. 'Yes.'

The garda says, 'I'm sorry for your loss.'

There's not much more to say than that.

Julie asks, 'When can I have him home?'

Hagan tells her, 'Today.'

She nods.

'Have you spoken with an undertaker?'

She nods. 'Mister Grogan.'

'I know him well,' he says. 'He'll take care of everything from here and contact you about the arrangements.' He doesn't tell her that he knows Grogan because he took care of Molly's funeral.

Julie nods.

Hagan draws the curtain closed, and Julie breaks down again, puts her hands on the glass and lets out a howl that can be heard throughout the whole morgue.

# CHAPTER NINE

IT'S BEEN EIGHT months and two weeks since Molly passed away, and the Coroner has concluded her investigation. Hagan is parked up on the nose of Howth Head, with the unopened envelope containing the Coroner's findings unopened. He watches Ireland's Eye slowly disappear into the darkness while the distant flashes of silent lightning slash across the horizon. Tired rumbles of muted thunder lag along. Counting the time between the flash and the thunder, he guesses it'll be some hours before the storm makes landfall. This spot on the edge of his world is where he was happiest as a boy, descending surefooted down the secret, dangerous cliff path to reach one of the prized outcrops of rocks that offered the best casting point to fish from. He closes his eyes to dwell in a happy boyhood memory full of fast-flashing silver, green, and blue striped mackerel that bite on bright red and yellow feathers, and he is lured to sleep. He dreams of dangerous beasts that lurk unseen in the dark waters. A boom of thunder shudders him awake. The violent rain whips the dark world all around him. The ambulance shudders in the heart-stopping buffeting. For a moment, he is a creature like any other at the mercy of the chaotic universe. Something fearful and primal hunkers down in him. He starts the engine, puts on the headlights, and is suddenly immune from the fear of the dark storm that dances harmlessly in front of him like a noisy drunk. He puts the engine into drive and proceeds down the steep, winding road through Howth Village and along the coast road through Sutton, Portmarnock, Malahide and Coolock to arrive home. It's silent in the house and colder inside than outside because he hasn't bothered to put the heating on.

Molly sits at the kitchen table as he comes in. 'Do you have it?'

'Yes.'

'I feel like I'm waiting on my leaving cert results.'

He moves to the sink and puts on the kettle. 'I don't think we would want to go through that again.'

'Have you read it yet?'

'No.'

'Why not?'

He doesn't want to read it because he understands the consequences of learning the truth. He intended not to read it unless Molly asked him. He didn't want to disturb her if she was at peace. But she is not at peace. She is here in the kitchen. Sitting at the table. Waiting.

He says, 'I wanted to wait until I was at home with a cup of tea.' He flicks the kettle on, comes to the table, and sits. 'Do you want me to read it?'

'Yes.' She's definite.

He removes the large brown A4 envelope from his pocket, carefully opens it, withdraws the document and begins reading it.

'What does it say?'

'It says that you died by accident.'

'What does that mean? I fell? What kind of accident?'

He focuses on the findings. 'Accidental overdose. There were drugs in your system and –'

'I've never taken drugs. You know that.'

'I know…'

'Then how can there be drugs found in my system?'

'I don't know.' But that's not true. He's seen plenty of instances of drugs turning up in the toxicology of young people who have no history of drug taking. 'Actually. I do know. You were spiked.'

'Yeah?'

'What do you remember?'

'Nothing. I was at the party. Dancing. I got dizzy. The rest is a blank.'

'That's a big gap in the narrative.'

'What about the person who called the ambulance?' She asks.

He scans the document, 'Let's see. Some witnesses. Other people from the party. They all say basically the same thing. You were in good spirits, having fun, and you disappeared. They thought you went home.'

Molly asks him again, 'But what about the person who made the call for the ambulance?'

'I'm looking. Looking... Let me see... Timeline. Ambulance arrives ... Attempted resuscitation. Unsuccessful. Pronounced dead on scene. The pathologist notes that you had several seizures before help arrived and suffered a massive bleed on the brain.'

'But what about the person who found me - who called the ambulance?'

He searches the paperwork. 'There's no record of who called the ambulance.'

'But that's not normal. Is it?'

'No. No, it's not normal.'

'There must be a record of it. Right.'

'Yes.'

She waits and watches him.

'I know where I can find the name.'

It's four in the morning when Hagan arrives at the City Morgue, makes his way to the Coroner's administration office, to three desks heaped with files that form an island in the middle of a small room walled with stuffed shelves – a place of limbo for paperwork. Most of these cases are closed and waiting to be moved into permanent storage, but they can spend up to two years in this hiatus because they could still be requested as evidence if the person convicted on the evidence within them appeals. He scans the piles of files, locates Molly's file, opens it, and flicks through the pages: the pathologist's report, the garda report, a half dozen handwritten witness statements, and the call answering division's original printout of the call log that contains the caller's mobile number, but no name is given. However, also in the file is a photocopy of the notes from the notebook of the first uniformed Garda on the scene, who questioned the man who found the body and recorded his name as Harry Murphy.

Hagan moves to the Coroner's computer, logs into the Justice Department's system, and runs a check on Harry Murphy to see if he has any previous convictions. The system takes a few seconds to run through the files and then responds with a file containing Murphy's previous convictions for the possession of drugs, his mugshot and his address, and a flag alerting any Gardai coming into contact with Murphy to contact the Organised Crime Unit.

'The OCU?' his head spins. Why was Murphy's name kept out of the report? The penny drops. 'He's a controlled informer…' He opens his notebook and begins writing Murphy's address into it.

Molly says, 'But … isn't Gallagher in the OCU?'

'Yes…'

'So she must know about Murphy.'

'Yes.'

'So what now?'

'Now … I'm going to do my due diligence on Harry Murphy and then pay him a visit.'

# CHAPTER TEN

THE SUN'S HUNGRY heat penetrated the drawn blackout curtains, filling the dark bedroom with thick, drowsy air. Hagan floated up from his deep sleep, listening to Molly singing her new morning regime that'd been in place since she began drama college. 'A E I O U' was sung up and down the scales. Vowel sounds, she explained. But it sounded to him like a long-forgotten language full of ancient secrets as she infused the air with her voice, clean and clear and full of determination. It filled his entire being with wellness.

She stopped. He listened out for the next part. After a moment of expectant silence, she began singing a fast fistful of words, knotted in a tight jumble at opposing angles to each other. 'To sit in solemn silence on a dull dark dock in a pestilential prison with a life-long lock awaiting the sensation of a short sharp shock from a cheap and chippy chopper on a big black block!' Repeating the words faster and faster, until she reached the correct speed, and somehow, the words magically flowed into a rhythm, filling the house with ambitious life as he made his way down to the kitchen and started the eggs.

She arrived as he put two perfectly timed soft-boiled eggs in their cups and placed them on the table next to a side plate of well-buttered soldiers, 'Here we go.'

'Thanks, Dad. Lovely.' She got stuck in, taking the top off the egg with surgical precision and dipping the soldiers into the soft yoke. 'What d'you think of my new vocal warm-up?'

'Bit gruesome.'

'It's from The Mikado.'

'The biscuit?'

'Funny … It's a musical. We should listen to it sometime. It's good. You'll like it.'

He came back to the kitchen table with mugs of tea. 'So it's all going well then?'

'Missus Rigby, my voice coach, says I should be thinking about musicals. Listening more to what I like. I have a great range, she says.'

'That's good.'

'She says I might even think about doing some auditions in London.'

'Wow. London.' He briefly thought London was too big and too far away for his little girl to go to and then reminded himself that she was nineteen. 'Sounds great.'

'I know that would be expensive and –'

'Don't worry about that.'

'Really?'

'Really. How's everything else?'

She shrugged and sipped her tea. 'I don't get some of it. You know?'

'Right. Like what?'

'The Shakespeare stuff. It's like … a different language.'

'I thought that monologue you recorded the other day was very good.'

'Really?'

'You sounded beautiful too.'

'Sounded beautiful?'

He tried to put it a better way. 'What do I mean? You sounded … passionate.'

She smiled. 'I'll take that.'

'And even though I didn't know what all the words meant – I knew what it was about.'

'What d'you mean?'

'Well. Most of the communication between people is nonverbal, isn't it? You know – like people unconsciously read each other's body language and tone of voice regardless of the words they're saying.'

'Did you read that?'

'I picked it up on the job.' He winked.

'You should come in and do some teaching.'

He smiles.

'You'd be better than the eejit we have teaching us Stanislavski.'

'Is he foreign?'

'From Galway.'

'He sounds foreign with that name.'

'The teacher? No wait. The teacher's name is Burke. Stanislavski is this Russian professor or something who created the method of acting. That's what they call it. The Method. I think.'

'Ah. Now I get you.'

'Does my head in. '

He studied her for a moment. 'Listen. I don't know anything about acting, but I know one thing – you can teach technique, but you can't teach talent. You either have it or you don't. You have it. In buckets.'

'Dad.'

'You were born with it. Got it from your mother.'

The front door opened, and Val called out like an actor, alerting the audience that she was about to enter from the wings, 'I'm home.'

Molly shook her head. 'Right on cue.'

She shared a conspiratorial smile with her father as Val entered the kitchen with gusto and went straight into her opening monologue. 'I got stuck talking to Missus Dunne about her new hip. The woman was oblivious to the flippin time ticking by. I think she's on pain medication or steroids or something. I didn't want to be rude. Ended up fibbing to her that I had something in the oven. She's off for a five-k-walk, she says. I says, in this heat? She says the heat doesn't bother her, that her great-grandfather was a Spaniard. I let her go before she started getting into her family history. We'd be there till sundown. Good luck to her. Off she went in a quick march. The bionic woman they're calling her now.' She glided to the teapot, and felt the side of it. 'How long is this standing?'

'Few minutes. It's fresh,' Hagan told her.

'Not very hot though,' she said.

He said, 'I don't put the water on the leaves at boiling point. Kills the flavour instead of releasing it. It's at drinking temperature.'

Val looked at Molly. 'Feckin history channel lecture on tea.'

Molly smiled. 'Dad, you could do a Ted Talk on making tea.'

Hagan didn't know what a Ted Talk was, but he knew it wasn't anything nasty if Molly said it. 'Thanks.'

Val poured the tea into the cup and eyed it with disappointment. 'And it's weak looking.'

Hagan defended his tea. 'You don't want it to be too overwhelming on the palate.'

'Stop,' she said, 'Please. It's lovely,' and made an aside to Molly, 'Really.'

But Hagan wasn't about to be the straight man for Val's routine. He said, 'It's like if you put too much chilli pepper into the chilli con carne. You can't actually taste any of the other ingredients because your mouth is filled with the sensation of burning.'

Val examined that. She knew he was having a go at her chilli con carne. She was about to remind him that his mother couldn't cook to save her life and that he didn't know what good food was until he came round to her mother's for the Sunday roast.

Molly sensed the change in the ether and moved into the middle of it to defuse them and asked her mother, 'How was choir?'

Val left the chilli con carne topic, but she would be coming back to it later in great detail, and Hagan knew it. She said to Molly, 'It was grand. Susan Farrell still thinks she's some kind of leading singer or something. A Diva. She's gone completely delusional now and is talking about entering herself into the A Star Is Born singing competition. I don't know how much longer Father John is going to put up with her. He keeps waving his finger at her to sotto voce, but she keeps on belting it out like she's doing an aria in an opera.' She sipped the tea and made a little grimace at it.

Hagan pretended not to see her face.

Molly kept it moving along in an orderly fashion. 'Getting kicked out of the choir. That will be a bit rough on her.'

Val thought for a moment, considering the loveliness of watching Susan Farrell getting the boot from the choir, but knew it would not happen. 'I don't think Father John would kick her out, so to speak. Maybe just put her at the back or something. She's not content to be up in the front row, but now she's started to take two steps forward so that she is out on her own. The woman's ego knows no bounds.'

Molly nodded. 'I know the type. Remember that one in Annie?'

Val waved her hand. 'Don't go there. And they made her your understudy? I went to the director and said, do you not realise that that girl's mother would pay someone to break my daughter's legs so that her daughter could step into the part of Annie?'

Molly laughed. 'You did not!'

'Of course I did. Sure, didn't it happen with that ice-skating girl, Tonya Harding? Your one, Kerrigan, got someone to break the poor girl's leg so that she could get to the Olympics. You have to watch your back.'

'I have you for that,' Molly said.

Val smiled.

'And dad,' Molly said.

Val sipped her tea again. The offence of the chilli insult was still stinging her. 'Hmm. Definitely too weak for me.' She flicked on the kettle. 'I'll make a fresh pot.' The kettle started to rumble right away. 'Anyway. What were you two talking about?'

'I don't know,' said Molly. 'What was it?'

'Stan somebody or other,' he said.

'Stanislavski!'

Val was not impressed. 'Have they got a half-decent tap and jazz teacher in yet?' She poured more hot water into the teapot and lobbed in two spoonfuls of tea leaves. 'Better.'

Hagan grimaced.

'What?' Val asked him.

'That's the Darjeeling that you've put in on top of the Earl Grey.'

Val looked at the line of tea caddies that he'd assembled along the counter. 'Why have you got six different kinds of tea?'

He began to explain in a purposefully slow fashion, like an expert tea witness giving his testimony to a jury full of coffee drinkers. 'The first is Earl Grey, then Lady Grey, then Darjeeling, then Breakfast Tea, then that lovely black China tea, and the green tea…'

She said, 'You know that's not normal. Right?'

Molly policed the situation again and said, 'No sign of the new teacher.'

Val poured the concoction of Breakfast and Darjeeling tea into the cup with purpose. 'That Stanislavski stuff is a con, I swear to God. Old rope. Live the life of your character? What do you do if you're playing a murderer? Go out and kill someone? Stupid. How are you all going to compete with the kids coming out of the London stage schools who can already dance the routines to every musical number out there?'

Molly said, 'There's talk about going over for open auditions.'

'Not yet,' Val said quickly, cutting the air with a warning finger. 'You'll only get one chance to make an impression with these casting directors. I know what they're like.'

'For the experience, they were saying.'

Val shook her head. 'No. No. You don't need experience in doing auditions. You've been doing them since you were four years old. Let the rest of them be cannon fodder in the cattle calls. We'll need to be smarter than that.'

'Right…' Molly knew better than to get into it with her mother. She seemed to have an elaborate, mysterious plan in her head that surfaced every now and then. There was no denying that Val knew her way around the bottom end of the entertainment industry. Molly respected that.

Val sipped her tea and pretended it was lovely and just how she liked it. 'Now.'

Hagan let her know that he could see through the rouse and said, 'There's lemon in the fridge if you need it.'

'I don't need lemon,' Val said and looked at the buttered soldiers piled up on Molly's plate and asked her husband, 'Do you think you put enough butter on those soldiers?'

He shrugged. 'Best bit.'

'I like butter,' Molly said. She wasn't taking sides, but she wasn't going to let her mother dictate what she should and should not eat. Those days were over.

Val looked at her. 'What about the cows? What your friend was saying?'

'Deirdre?'

'Yeah.'

Molly shrugged. 'That's her deal. Not mine. I like butter.'

Val nodded. She knew she should let it go and move on, but sometimes it was like she didn't have control over the stuff she said, like she had to be cruel to be kind. 'And the butter likes you. Once it goes into you, it doesn't want to leave.' She expertly manoeuvred from the position of accuser into sympathiser. 'Believe me.' She patted her hips. 'The struggle is real.'

Molly unconsciously ran her hand over her dress. Maybe she needs to be more strict with herself. 'I know.'

Val became almost consoling. 'I'm only saying. You know, you'll be starting to go to proper auditions now. You know what they're like, and you're not a little girl anymore.'

Hagan felt his hackles involuntary rise. 'I don't think she needs to be worrying about any of that.'

Val picked up the crumpled tea towel, flicked it out, and folded it into order. 'Well, it's nice that you think that, but I can tell you, the reality is very different for a woman. I wish I had someone who knew what they were talking about when I was starting out.'

Hagan and Molly waited for one of Val's stories about any number of narrowly missed opportunities into stardom. 'I was called back three times for The Patriots. Three. The director, Alan Marker, couldn't get enough of me. Thought I was great. The casting agent, Rozzie, said no one could match me on the voice. Little did I know that the dress size was already chosen by the producers and –.'

Molly's phone buzzed with a text alert, breaking the flow of the story.

'Sorry.' Molly checked her phone. Took a sharp breath. Held her hand in the air like she had received a message from God. 'Wait a minute. Stop. No way.'

'What?' Val moved closer.

'I think I have an agent.'

Val put her mug down in case she dropped it. 'What?' Then took a breath.'Who?'

'The Chase Agency. I sent in that showreel I made and a CV and… '

Val sat. 'Oh my God. What does it say? What?'

Molly read it out, 'Loved your showreel. Let's make an appointment to talk. Jeff.'

Val tapped the table. 'Jeff? That's Jeffery Chase. He texted you himself?'

'That's what it says.'

Val hugged Molly.

Hagan looked on, smiling, happy that Val and Molly were at one.

# CHAPTER ELEVEN

IT'S A BEAUTIFUL day for a picnic as Hagan drives his old Skoda Octavia with half a million miles on it along a narrow old country road. 'We used to come up here when I was in the Boy Scouts. Up to the pine forest,' he says.

Molly smiles. 'I didn't know you were in the scouts.'

'Dyb. Dyb. Dyb.'

'What does that even mean?'

'Do your best.'

'I like that.'

Dublin can change from suburb to wilderness at the turn of a corner. Five minutes after exiting the busiest motorway in the country, He's is in the leafy green environs of Ferndale where every winding road becomes a private boreen leading to a dead end punctuated with an emphatic big black gate, a CCTV camera and a sign nailed to a tree like a crucified Christian warning you that you're in a neighbourhood watch zone; a reminder that strangers are not welcome here. The big houses behind the lines of big trees are under siege from an invisible but insatiable enemy of curious suburbanites. He drives by the gate of Murphy's house without stopping, checking the level of security: two cameras and three signs declaring private property. He's not going to get to Murphy through his front gate.

Last night, he sat up with Molly, examining the area on a satellite view, which showed that Murphy's gated property backs into a sloping hill that then quickly turns into a heavily wooded area at the foot of the Dublin mountains, and in that wood, rambling through it like an artery, is a walker's path. He now has the bones of a plan that will give him the time alone with Murphy that he needs to interrogate him properly about his involvement in Molly's death. Arriving at the mountain carpark, he sees three other cars parked up and a few muddy ramblers peeling out of their boots, and drives to the far corner and parks up. 'Let's go for a walk.'

'Lovely.'

With a small haversack over his shoulder, he sets off on the path into silence, into the heart of the forest. A little bit along the path, the canopy closes overhead, and the sounds of the world around him become muted. Unseen creatures move about, and a dormant part of his brain switches on to hunt mode; even though the knowledge and skills have been lost from his bloodline hundreds of years ago, the instinct is still there in the same way that a domestic house dog might remember something of being a wolf, and even dream of running with the pack. The cold air feels good as he draws it deep into his hot lungs. Molly cuts in front of him, impatient. He notices she's wearing a long black coat that reaches to the ground.

'Where did you get that coat?'

'Nana gave it to me.'

He has no memory of his mother ever wearing the coat.

Molly says, 'It belongs to her mother.'

He now remembers seeing that coat in an old picture of his grandmother. 'Are they all where you are?'

'No. But I can come and go to them whenever I want and come to you whenever I want. Or to Mam.'

'Mam?'

'She doesn't see me. But she knows when I'm close to her. But … it makes her cry. I don't want to make her cry. Maybe you could explain it to her.'

'I'll try…'

She says, 'When you get to Murphy?'

'Yes.'

'Promise me you won't … you won't be brutal.'

He won't make a promise to Molly that he can't keep. 'I promise you that I won't hurt him unless I have to … and if I have to, then I won't hurt him any more than I need to.'

She thinks about that. 'That's good. If he's guilty, they want you to send him to them.' 'I'll send him.'

76

'Maybe he will be innocent.'

'Maybe.'

Further, along the path, the forest canopy thins out, and the sun cuts into the interior in bright shafts that capture the pollen clouds and busy insects buzzing within it. He is filled with wellness and feels he could stop and watch the show all day, let the world just go on without him, but he's also aware that he's experiencing an endorphin rush, a pleasant side effect of the painkillers. Focusing, he checks his compass and cuts from the path to find the spot he saw on the satellite view of Murphy's property.

'Time for some tea.'

An old stump makes a perfect seat to sit and sip tea and examine the property through binoculars. He's happy to see that there's no fencing around the house; it's impossible to see where Murphy's property stops and the public lands of the Dublin Mountains begin. The layout of the building is odd, and it's hard to tell if it started as a house or a barn. But if he is to be successful here, then he must figure it out.

The primary role of the Boy Scout movement was to train boys to be useful in war, to carry messages, and to gather intelligence. A scout must know how to survive on the land, build shelter, hunt, navigate, read and draw maps. But it is most important to be able to draw accurate diagrams of enemy installations such as trench formations, forward observational posts, barracks and encampments. He begins sketching Murphy's house.

'You're very good at that,' she tells him.

'I like drawing. I'm trying to get a sense of the layout inside from the bone structure.'

The building is two structures, a house and a barn, that have been awkwardly joined together. The entire back wall is made of glass and covered by heavy curtains. Beyond that, it's impossible to be sure what's inside, but the interior has likely been gutted and made into an open plan. With binoculars, he searches along the walls. 'No security cameras.'

She says, 'People are here.'

'What you lookin at there?' a male voice with an American accent asks from behind him.

Hagan looks around to see two elderly tourists who don't look like they should be rambling around a forest. The man nods to the binoculars that Hagan has in his hand.

Hagan says, 'Nesting blue tits.'

Molly giggles.

The man says, 'Wow. That's awesome. Blue Tits. We got cardinals in our yard back home.'

The woman says, 'We got a feeder out there for them.'

The man says, 'Brings them right in close where we can see them.'

The woman says, 'But we also got squirrels who raid the feeder.'

The man says to the woman, 'I hope Joe remembers to keep that feeder full while we're on vacation.'

'He will,' the woman says.

The man says, 'You know, the feeder runs dry then they go someplace else.'

The woman says, 'They won't go no place else.'

The two of them stare out at the landscape. 'Wow,' says the man.

The woman says, 'It's so green.'

The man says, 'It's a very peaceful spot right here, isn't it, honey?'

'It sure is,' the woman agrees.

The man says to Hagan, 'We were walking up there on the track and spotted you.'

Hagan nods.

Next activity on the list is taking pictures. The phones come out, and they ask Hagan if he wouldn't mind taking a picture of them.

He obliges.

The woman asks Hagan, 'Hey, can we get one of you with us?'

The man doubles down on the request. 'So we can tell them about the guy we met looking at blue tits.'

They share a little giggle about that. Ireland is great. Full of strange characters.

Hagan says, 'Unfortunately, I have a terrible phobia of having my picture taken.'

They examine him for a moment.

The man says, 'I hear you, man.'

The woman says, 'That must be awful for you.'

Hagan says, 'I've learned to live with it, but it ruined by modelling career.'

After a moment, they laugh.

The woman says, 'I think Ralphie has that.'

The man says, 'Little Ralphie?'

They begin a discussion about little Ralphie.

Hagan makes his exit. 'It was nice meeting you. Enjoy your holiday.'

They nod and smile and then turn their attention to the fabled blue tit that's out there somewhere.

'What does it look like?' The woman says.

'I guess it's blue.' The man says.

They scan the sky, the bushes, and the general environs.

Hagan walks back with Molly to the carpark that is about a half mile away and sees a coach driver waiting with a coach full of pissed-off-looking people.

'You didn't happen to run into two Americans up there, did you?' the driver asks Hagan.

'I did. They've stopped for a bit of birdwatching.'

The driver looks at his watch. 'Jesus.'

A woman comes to the coach's door with a face frozen in surprise and anger. She says, 'We're all waiting here.' Then she glares at Hagan like he is supposed to do something about it.

Molly says, 'There's no need for you to stand here being polite, Dad. C'mon.'

Hagan walks to his car, gets in and drinks a cup of tea from his flask. Molly sits in the passenger seat. She says, 'It'll be dark soon.'

'Yes.'

Fifteen minutes later, the two rambling Americans appear down the hill, regaling everyone on the bus with their great adventure up in the woods.

When the bus has left the car park, Hagan walks back and forth two more times to the spot that overlooks the house, memorising it so that he can walk it in the dark.

Molly says, 'You don't like to leave anything to chance, do you?'

'The way I see it,' he says, 'there's always going to be things outside your control. So you better control the things you can. Getting lost up here in the dark is something that I can avoid.'

After his fourth trip up and down the path, he exits the carpark and drives further up into the mountains, finds a lay-by and takes a few painkillers.

'When I'm dealing with him,' he says, 'I don't want you there.'

She looks at him for a moment. 'Fine. But remember what you promised.'

He nods. 'I won't hurt him unless I have to, and if I have to, no more than I need to. Promise.'

She nods.

He reclines his seat and closes his eyes.

She sits quietly, gazing out into the brooding mountains while he snoozes. Night fog comes in around them and blankets the mountains in darkness.

Three hours later, he wakes fully rested and eager. She's not there. Returning to the carpark at the forest trail, he parks the car. He removes his backpack that contains a packet of surgical wipes, an ice pick, pliers, a surgical cutting knife, a forensic jumpsuit, a mask, a pair of safety goggles, a half dozen pairs of latex gloves, a heavy-duty plastic bag, a roll of heavy-duty duct tape and a bag of cable ties. He sets off into the dark along the memorised path. The frost has set in with the night, making the ground hard and covering it in a wafer-thin layer of ice that crunches under his feet. He's glad it's cold because a rising surge of adrenaline is making him hot, but he feels good. More than that, he feels great, like he's in a perfect moment, doing what he needs to do; it feels natural to be hunting for revenge in the darkness. Free from the light of day, he's freed from the social conditioning that convinces a man to go to war and kill on command but at the same time tells him that he doesn't have the right to kill for personal revenge, tells him that he must give up that right to the State that may or may not act for him. And if the courts should decide that the man's enemy is to walk free, then the civilised man must accept it. Hagan has seen enough guilty people walking away from justice as the families of the victims look on from the gallery, obediently following the law that's not serving them, being civilised. Fuck being civilised.

He puts on a balaclava and gloves, carefully making his way down the hill to the hedge that probably marks a land boundary, and goes through it to see the house is in darkness. There's a surprising amount of animal activity: foxes, badgers, owls, and other nocturnal creatures busy hunting or being hunted. Every so often, things go quiet as they get a whiff of the human, but when the animals don't smell a dog as well, they go back to their business. He's a complete novice at breaking and entering, but he got lots of advice on the subject from the internet. The best advice was to take things slowly and constantly remind himself that he knows nothing of the craft. However, on the flip side, he's an enthusiastic DIY man and knows his way around window latches and door frames. You could say he has a skill set that he can apply here.

Murphy's social media says he's single and always ready to mingle. And judging by his online photo album, that Hagan viewed and downloaded, Murphy seems to party for a living. Hagan took care not to leave a digital trail on the internet and took the precaution of using a virtual private network to protect his identity. He's also left his phone at home plugged into the charger. He's had a front-row seat to criminality for twenty years and knows how people get caught and how they get away with it, too.

Carefully, he takes the small crowbar from the bag. Every piece of kit in the bag is new, and he's never touched any of it with his bare hands. This particular crowbar scored very high on a burglary website that he found on the darknet. There were also lots of instructional videos and some tutorials on lock breaking. Turns out that *"of all the locks in the world, the sliding patio door lock is probably the most ineffectual. There's insufficient frame on the thin, lightweight structure to house a sturdy bolt. It's a perfect example of form over function in the battle between being a window and a door. It cannot be both. Front doors are built to keep out Viking hoards. Back doors are built to keep out the draft. Patio doors are not doors; they're just big windows."* There was also a beneficial tutorial video on how to deal with patio door locks. As instructed, He eases the chiselled edge of the crowbar's claw between the space where the two patio doors meet. It's unnerving how easily it gives way. He eases the sliding door open and gently pushes through the heavy curtains.

*"Creeping is the term used for being inside the property that you're burglarising"* the burglar with the most likes explained. *"When you're creeping, you need to stop and close your eyes so as to let your other senses come into the game."*

As he puts his head into the dark interior, he hears the long, steady grunt of snoring from a deep sleeper. Stepping softly into the dark room, he closes the curtain behind him. He's never felt more alive. Every fibre of his body tingles. It is a primal exhilaration to be in the layer of your sleeping enemy. He must calm down. He breathes deeply. His senses are amped all the way up. He smells everything: food, weed, smelly feet, cologne. His eyes search into the dark, but he must follow the advice from the online burglary tutorial and counterintuitively close his eyes. He forces his eyelids shut and feels a shot of raw fear shoot through his veins like ice water.

Then, a surge of something that he just doesn't have a name for because he has never felt anything like it, but it gives him an erection like he hasn't had since he was a teenager. He expects to be hit in the face by his unseen enemy, but he must keep his eyes closed to force his other senses into overdrive. In a moment, he is calm. He hears everything: the night moving against the outside of the house, the air moving inside of it, his pumping heart, his rushing blood, and the jagged snores sawing the perfect silence... After a moment, he reckons the direction the snoring is coming from. He tunes out the sound of his rapidly beating heart and the rush of blood in his ears. His mind floats in the dark and follows the snoring that seems to be coming from above him. He opens his eyes, now accustomed to darkness, and begins to make out a world of charcoal shapes.

The strange plan of the house space could be a shop that displays various pieces of furniture in no particular order. Two couches join together in the middle of the open space, facing the glass wall that looks out onto the mountains. In the far corner is an armchair with a reading lamp next to it. Moving through the dark, he follows the sound of the snoring to the mezzanine floor above, climbing the metal spiral staircase, he finds Murphy sprawled naked upon an enormous bed. Next to the bed is an array of drugs on a small bedside table.

He gently places Murphy's feet side by side, sliding a cable tie around each ankle so they are looped together. There's no need to pull them tightly into place because when Murphy tries to move his legs, the bindings will close tight like a snare trap. For a moment, He is reminded of his days in the scouts when they tried unsuccessfully to snare a rabbit. Their old scout leader, who'd been active in the jungle warfare of Burma, explained how the snares were also good traps for the enemy along the path and pointed out that if you kill an enemy, then his body is left in place by his comrades, but if you injure him, then his comrades must carry him, and this way you can slow them down and tire them out.

'Wake up,' he says.

The snoring stops. Stutters. Starts again.

Interrogation was another subject that Hagan knew next to nothing about. But thankfully, he found an Onion website that covered the craft in great detail. Most of the tutorial was written by an interrogator who worked in Guantanamo Bay and had many years of experience in non-fatal torture techniques. *"If you kill your prisoner, the information dies with them,"* he pointed out at the outset of his tutorial video. Hagan was surprised to learn that hope was the most useful tool in the interrogator's toolbox. *"The prisoner must always believe that he will be allowed to go free if he gives up the information."*

He says louder, 'Harry Murphy. Wake up.'

The snoring stops, followed by a dead silence. Murphy stays still, not breathing for a second, as he realises that someone is at the foot of his bed. He takes a deep, fearful breath and jumps out of bed, involuntarily pulling the ankle restraints tight, and falls flat on his face on the floor and belly crawls fast like a man transformed into a snake – slithering to the corner.

Hagan knows he can't let Murphy reach the weapon he's desperately crawling to. He kneels on his back and places the wriggling man in a chokehold. 'Easy now. Easy.'

Murphy struggles and panics, reaching blindly into the dark.

Hagan says, 'I just want to talk to you.'

Murphy stops struggling. He already knows that this man is too strong to fight hand-to-hand. 'What? What? D'you want?'

Hagan says, 'Come on now. If I wanted to kill you, you'd be dead already. Relax.'

Murphy's mind spins through the possibilities: is it a robbery? 'I have about two hundred grand cash. You can have it, and there's a fresh kilo of pure coke and—'

'I'm not here to rob you.'

'What then?'

Hagan keeps Murphy face down. 'Hands behind your back.'

'Are you a cop?'

'Hands behind your back.'

*"Be clear with your instructions; establish dominance quickly."*

Hagan takes Murphy's right hand, brings it around, and places a cable tie on it. Murphy doesn't resist as the second hand is brought behind his back, and the second cable is looped through the first to form handcuffs.

'Don't pull against them,' Hagan says, 'They will just get tighter and cut off the blood supply to your hands.' *"Take an early opportunity to bond with his prisoner."* 'I don't want you to hurt yourself.'

The Interrogator underlined the importance of this bonding process. *"You should come across as a man just doing his job. Don't ever show any pleasure in your task."*

'Please tell me what you want?' Murphy says.

'I already told you. I just want to talk.' Hagan takes him by the shoulders and hauls him to a chair. 'Let's sit up here.'

He lifts Murphy with such ease that it makes Murphy feel like he's a corpse.

Once Murphy is sitting in the chair, Hagan stands in front of him and lets him see that he is wearing a mask.

*"The mask is another important tool of the interrogation plan because it allows the prisoner to think that he is going to leave the interrogation alive. After all, you don't have to hide your face from a guy you're going to kill, right?"*

Hagan then daisy-chains four of the foot-long cable ties, creating a loop around the back of the chair and Murphy's torso, and tightens it just enough.

Murphy starts making nervous chatter, 'Whatever you want to know. Just ask. Ask.'

*"Compliance in the interrogation is a double-edged sword for the interrogator. Most of the time, it's babble, and the prisoner will say anything that comes into his head to fill the silence. It's important to build structure into the session and start with questions that have definite answers, answers that can be proven quickly."*

Hagan moves to the corner that Murphy was trying to get to. 'What's over here?'

'A gun.'

'Where?'

'Bottom drawer.'

Hagan opens the bottom drawer of the dresser, shines the slender beam of the pencil torch into it and sees the gun along with an enormous stash of various drugs. He leaves it untouched and returns to Murphy. *"It's important to reward the prisoner when he tells the truth."* 'Thank you for telling me that. I appreciate it.'

Murphy nods. 'Take what you want.'

'I'm not a thief. Now listen. Here's how this will work.'

*"Establishing the ground rules is the next most important part of the interrogation."*

'I'm not a sadist. I don't want to hurt you if I don't have to. I'll ask questions. If you answer them, no problem. I get the truth, and I go away.'

*"You need to set out the carrot."*

'Listen, man, I don't know who you are, but that gear in that drawer is worth about a million and—'

*"And the stick."*

'Stop talking and listen. Now. The important bit. If you don't answer my questions truthfully, I will hurt you.'

'I don't even–'

'Listen.' Hagan waits. 'Focus. If I have to hurt you, it won't be like slaps or digs or even breaking your fingers. It will be pain like you can't even imagine. Do you understand that?'

'I don't know you, man. What the fuck? What's this about?'

'I need to hear to say that you understand me about the pain. Say it.'

'Fuck. Yes. I understand you. What do you want to know?'

Hagan shines the torch into Murphy's eyes.

Murphy squints and looks away from the light.

'No. Look into the light,' Hagan says.

Murphy does as he's told. 'Just fuckin–'

'No more talking,' Hagan says. 'You only talk to answer questions now. That's it. Look into the light.'

Murphy looks into the light and Hagan watches the pupils of his eyes adjust and shrink, just like the interrogator said they would.

'Nine months ago … You called an ambulance for a girl who was found in a laneway. Correct?' Hagan stops talking and watches Murphy's eyes fill with the memory of the scene.

'Yeah…'

'How did you find her?'

Hagan watches Murphy's eyeballs flit around. According to the Interrogator, *"Flitting eyeballs is a sign that the prisoner is searching for a lie, and the only reason to lie is to protect the truth. If your question was pertinent to their involvement in a crime, this is a clear sign that you are on the right track."*

Hagan knows that the flitting eyeballs are not the action of a good samaritan who found a young girl in a lane and tried to help. The adrenaline hitting Murphy's bloodstream causes his pupils to expand.

*"When the prisoner is in fear, his eyes will open right up, regardless of the light."*

'I was out for the night...' Murphy begins.

Hagan knows that this will be a preamble to lying.

*"This is the prisoner buying time to create a narrative. It is important to impose your will on the prisoner right here, to show him the consequences of lying."*

Murphy goes on, 'I was with my friends. It was a birthday party and–'

Hagan turns off the torch. Murphy stops talking and is blind now. Then he feels a strip of tape going across the mouth. He screams into the tape. He pulls against his bindings that tighten around fast. He keeps on screaming until he hears Hagan's voice.

'The pain will last for ten seconds.'

*"When you punish your prisoner, it is most important to be clinical and non-emotional and to deliver the punishment in a controlled fashion in a controlled environment for an allotted amount of time. A sample of short, sharp pain techniques is listed below."*

Hagan's knowledge of human anatomy allows him to choose a high-reward pain technique usually performed by someone with medical training. He takes Murphy's head into an armlock so that it can't move and, with his free hand, slides the ice pick into Murphy's jaw, through the muscles into the gum, under a molar, and past the root until he finds the lingual nerve. He knows when he's hit the sweet spot because Murphy's body goes into a rigid spasm of pain that seizes control of his brain. Hagan counts to ten and removes the ice pick. Murphy's body goes limp, and he weeps like a bereaved lover in great sobs and snots of grief.

*"It is important to reestablish contact with your prisoner after the pain. This is when he will be at his most vulnerable and see you, from this point on, in a different light now that you have proven your words."*

Hagan gives him a minute to recover, and then, following the advice of the Interrogator, he says, 'I'm sorry I had to do that. I don't want to hurt you like that again. Okay?'

Murphy nods.

Hagan removes the tape from his mouth. Waits.

Murphy continues to sob. Broken.

*"The lingual spike is guaranteed to break most ordinary prisoners straight out of the gate. Very few individuals are built to withstand repeated spiking. In the end, everyone always gives up the truth."*

Murphy now knows he is helpless to stop the pain beyond anything he ever imagined being inflicted upon him at will. He's lost all of his presumptions about who or what he is. He now feels no more than a simple animal for slaughter in a kill pen. All those mornings that the farmer came to the barn whistling and feeding him were just part of an elaborate plan to fatten him up and then betray him. He gets it now. The ego dies. But hope lives on. He talks like a repentant sinner in purgatory, confessing all his sins and hoping for a reprieve. 'I sell drugs … I'm a dealer. I have VIP clients. You know, music and movie and television people. That night, one of my clients … do you want names?'

'Yes.' Hagan waits with his notebook and pen at the ready. This part of the business wasn't in the interrogation and torture tutorial; it is part of his working methodology borne from years of meticulously documenting the dead.

'Jeff Chase,' Murphy says, 'He's an agent. He was having a party for his clients in the Bordello Club, it's a nightclub, but you know that right? Yeah. But Chase's parties are like … Have you heard of Bunga Bunga parties?'

'Yes.'

'Like that. Lots of drugs, lots of girls, lots of boys – all young wannabe models and actors and clients of Chase's talent agency. And lots of rich, influential men. They have this routine where they pick girls or guys and roofie them. You know what that is?'

'Yes.'

'Right, well, I was there that night, supplying the drugs. I got called upstairs to one of the rooms that they have there with a mattress on the floor. The girl was in there naked on the mattress, roofied off her head. But I could tell by looking at her that she'd fitted. Probably more than once. Her eyes were rolled right back in her head. She'd been there for a while. They wanted me to get her out of there.'

Hagan fights hard to keep the image of Molly out of his mind; he doesn't want the picture of her lying naked on a mattress and fitting from drugs, he doesn't want to cry, he doesn't want to explode and smash this man into pulp. He takes a breath and asks, 'They?'

'Well Chase was there and Marcus Strauss. He's a movie producer.'

Hagan writes the name into his book. 'Anyone else?'

'Doyle. The DJ.'

'Dennis Doyle?'

'Yeah.'

Hagan adds the name to his book. His hand sakes with temper. He fights to stay on it. 'Then what?'

'I wanted to call an ambulance right then and there. But, you know, they said I had to take her out to the back before I called it in.'

Hagan reminds himself that Molly is not beyond pain. He must calm his mind on focus. He can see the pool of piss that has formed under Murphy's chair, and he can get the smell of shit from him.

Murphy says, 'That's it.'

'You were just doing what you were told.'

'Yeah.'

'Why was your name redacted from the records?'

'I'm a garda informer.'

'And you didn't reach out to your garda handler or whatever?'

Murphy thinks about the pain he'll get for lying, and he knows he can't take it again. And why should he? Who's he protecting? He tells the truth. 'I made the call as soon as I knew about the girl.'

Hagan takes a moment before he asks the next question that he thinks he already knows the answer to. 'What is the name of the garda you called?'

'DS Helen Gallagher.'

This portion of truth is putrid and almost makes Hagan vomit. Gallagher was the first person to offer Hagan and Val her sympathies. She even went so far as to say she would conduct an off-the-record investigation into what happened to Molly and asked Hagan if he had any information. Now he knows she was just looking after the business of cleaning up the mess.

'What did Gallagher say to you?'

'Wait until the club is cleared out, then get the girl out to the back lane, and call it in then.'

Now, Hagan is asking questions that he doesn't want answers to but has to ask. 'How long did you wait before the club was empty?'

'About two hours.'

Two hours. Two fucking hours. The thoughts of his little girl lying and waiting for help for hours, naked and dying, release a poison into Hagan's bloodstream that finds any mercy he might have for the people who are responsible for Molly's death and kills it. He presses on because he must have all of the details.

'How did you move her?'

'Me and another fella dressed her and carried her out.'

'Who was the other fella?'

'Pike.'

'Pike?'

'Doyle's driver.'

Hagan writes the name into his notebook, closes it and puts it into his pocket. He's done here.

The Interrogator advised, "*Truth is dangerous. If a prisoner is keeping a truth that is deadly to him, and he tells you that truth, then that truth becomes deadly to you. Truth can set you on a road that you may not have intended to go on. Sometimes, the truth holds terrible consequences far beyond what you could have imagined.*"

Hagan knew before he came in here looking for the truth that he might get it, might learn that Molly's death was not an accident and that he would have to be prepared to act upon it. But he wasn't expecting to hear this. He walks behind Murphy.

'Is that it?' Murphy asks.

'Yes. It's over now.'

Murphy relaxes.

Hagan takes him in a headlock and quickly turns the head in a sharp clockwise direction, severing the connection between the cervical vertebrae C3 from C4 and thus tearing the spinal cord to cease communication between the brain and the vital organs. Death begins to occur immediately. The body goes through spasms as each organ fights for life; Hagan senses the terrified soul emerging from its corpse, and then all around him, the air fills with the presence of others, swirling, angry, violent, and Murphy's ripe soul is consumed.

Then all is still, they are gone, but for one soul that lingers, and Hagan recognises the stoic presence of his mother, reminding him that this is the beginning of his work, not the end. The next moment, he is in an empty house with a corpse. He should feel something. Satisfaction. Guilt. He feels nothing. He feels empty. Feeling emotions is a luxury he cannot afford right now because he is only three quarters ways through his killing. He once heard a senior Garda detective explain, *"The square of crime: Every crime, including murder, needs four elements: One, a motivated offender. Two, a suitable victim. Three, an opportunity to commit, and four, the means of escape."* Hagan needs to complete the square and escape capture because his work has only begun as an avenging father with an amount of killing yet to do.

Moving across the room, he examines the stash of drugs, a gun, and a large amount of cash and begins his staging of the scene to look like a robbery murder, pulling a heavy-duty plastic from his backpack and bagging up the stash. He then puts on his forensic suit, mask and gloves, retrieves another heavy-duty plastic bag and a surgical knife and removes the head from the corpse, placing it into the plastic bag. All that done, he gathers his equipment, the bag of stash and the bag with the head in it, and makes a tidy exit the same way he entered, leaving the sliding door open and a gap in the curtain to encourage fly infestation.

Walking up the hill, his limbs feel light, and his back is new again. His body is pumped with enough endorphins, adrenalin and testosterone to give most men of his age a heart attack, but he is elated in the night, and the darkness feels like his ally. The animals flitting about in the bushes don't shy from him. He's one of them now, walking in their world, in a universe free of complicated constructs to find reason and prove reality or magical thinking to justify his existence. He's simply an apex predator in a food chain where he can kill if he wants to. He's going to kill those named by Murphy. The rush of euphoria makes him dizzy. He stops and lies down on the earth on his back and allows the rush to come like a shot of pure liquid morphine. Up and up and up he goes until he feels like he might break through the stratosphere and enter space. Floating there on the edge of the earth's fragile bubble that holds the planet's delicate life in place, he looks out into the abyss, and in that moment, the abyss looks back at him and tells him that everything beyond here is desolation. He cannot stay for long at this breathless high altitude and must come down to earth. Removing the card of codeine pills from his pocket, he pops four white pellets from their beds and into his mouth and chews them. The slowing drugs slug through his veins and make him heavy, and gravity pulls him back down to the safety of the earth where he belongs. Back in his senses, he realises that if it were not for the killings he must do, he could stay right here and happily wait for his body to die and free his soul so that he could join Molly.

'Did you hurt him?' Molly asks.

'Not any more than I needed to.'

She sits beside him. She's wearing Nana Hagan's long black wool coat and carrying a long switch of hazel, cutting the air with it. The night and its inhabitants fall into an attentive silence like the first listeners sitting around the fire waiting to hear the story of the hunt.

'Why do you ask?'

'I heard him howling,' she says.

'He didn't howl,' he says.

'He howled. A lot.'

He says, 'Not in this world, he didn't.'

She nods. 'Nana told me they were going to take him and not to go in and look.'

'Nana knows best.' He asks, 'Who are "they"?'

She cuts the air with the switch. 'The ancient ones, Nana called them. The ones we come from, she said. A warrior people.' She cuts the air again with the switch. 'One of them gave me this.'

Hagan nods. 'We come from Vikings. They were a fierce people.'

'What did Murphy tell you?'

'He told me you were roofied and raped … and he gave me the names of the men who did it?'

'It was Jeffery Chase, wasn't it?'

'He was one of them.'

'I kind of knew it. Do you think that's why he took me onto his books?'

'What do you mean?'

'Like, when I got an agent, I thought it was because I was talented.'

'You had buckets of talent.'

'Then why…'

'Because these men are predators. It's their nature. Every young girl who comes into their world is a potential victim. Nothing you did made you any more or less of a victim. They created a perfect environment, filled it with potential victims and simply acted on the opportunity to commit their crime when it was presented to them.

Molly asks, 'What now?

He says, 'I'm going to kill them.'

# CHAPTER TWELVE

HAGAN DRIVES AT speed through the wet grey dawn under sirens and lights. Sleet comes sideways through the beams of the ambulance's headlights. Joe imagines that he's making reentry through Earth's atmosphere as they make their approach to a two-hundred-year-old pub plopped in the middle of a vast black tar carpark like a crannog in the middle of a bog lake. A herd of hooded teenagers gather in a clump against a wall that offers some protection from the elements, staring out into the gloom like young hopeless bullocks in a Cavan field, waiting for the slaughter man to come and put them out of their misery. They'd all rather be at home in their warm beds, but their gang boss has ordered them to turn out and make a show of force at the murder scene of their fellow gang member.

At the doors of the pub, a half dozen black-clad Gardai armed with machine guns stand ready to riddle anyone who comes looking for trouble. They'd also rather be home, but their boss ordered them out into the weather to stand at the crime scene and make a show of force for law and order.

The hooded heads turn in unison, watching the morgue ambulance reverse into a safe spot between a Garda van and the white Garda Technical Bureau van.

'Wait here until I come back,' Hagan tells Joe as he gets out and walks quickly into the pub.

Through the fogged window, Joe can see across the carpark to the gang of hoodies watching him like they've sniffed him out. A familiar schoolyard nausea begins to stir in the pit of his stomach as the bullies spot their prey. His phone vibrates and glows with a notification about a new post on Gangsta Rap. He opens it and looks to see a picture of himself sitting in the ambulance outside of the Outpost Pub, staring out of the window into the picture. The caption reads, *"The bodysnatchers have turned up. Look at the head on this retarded cunt."*

Hagan carefully enters the pub, the dark interior is mostly as it was in the 1800s when the old inn was a stopover for coaches to rest the horses and weary travellers on their way to and from the Capital. He spots the technical officers in pristine white jumpsuits, examining the area like alien creatures, trying to figure out what humans do in here all day and night. Detective Sergeant Helen Gallagher appears out of the dim and comes to him. 'We'll have to stop meeting like this. People will talk,' she jokes.

He nods and smiles, 'Busy night.'

'You still have Rory Keegan onboard?'

'I do.'

She touches her head like she's pretending that she's just thought of something. 'By the way. Did you happen to find a phone on him?'

Hagan nods and knows now that she wasn't on the scene of Rory Keegan's death by chance any more than she just chanced upon the scene of Molly's death. But he doesn't voice any of that.

'So you took it?' She makes a bad act of trying to hide how keen she is about the phone. It always amazes Hagan how bad cops are at subterfuge, considering they spend most of their working hours dealing with criminals.

'Was technically on the body. So yes,' he says.

'Couldn't have a quick look at it, could I?'

'Sure,' he says, 'I just have to make a quick call to the Coroner and get the okay.'

This stops her dead in her tracks. 'Jesus, no,' she says, 'Don't bother the Coroner.'

'It's not a bother.'

She looks around for nothing in particular. 'It was just a quick look I wanted.'

Hagan starts to politely tell her to go fuck herself. 'It's entered into the possessions docket. The Coroner just issued a reminder to us about the chain of evidence. We have an ongoing nightmare situation over the phone of a murdered gang member that was accessed without a court order, and its contents were used as evidence in a trial. It's going all the way to the high court. The conviction might be overturned because the evidence was inadmissible.'

'I heard that.' She says, as if she doesn't know every cough and spit of that case and examines him a little. 'You know a lot about that case then?'

'Meself and Old Frank removed the body from the prison cell. The phone was removed from the corpse's rectum at the morgue and logged into the evidence room. So I'm a witness because the chain of evidence was broken – somehow.'

'Not by you.'

'Not by me.' He doesn't tell her that Old Frank gave a detective access to the phone because he knows that she already knows.

'Old Frank is retired now, right?' She says.

Hagan nods.

She says, 'You know what? It's more trouble to me than it's worth. I'll get the court order signed and drop it into the morgue tomorrow.'

'Great.' Hagan is keen to get on with the job at hand, 'Where's the body?'

'In the snug,' she tells him with a grin. 'Messy.'

Hagan moves along the bar to the cosy compartment at the end of the room. The wooden floor is tacky with spilt beer and blood that makes the soles of his boots stick to it a little as he walks to the narrow, snug entrance. Sitting inside the snug is a large headless corpse surrounded by a violent crimson halo of blood, bone, and brain matter, like a headless baptist in the shrine of a blood sacrifice.

Gallagher says, 'Shot him point blank in the face with a double-barrelled sawn-off.

Both barrels. Took his head right off. So would you call that psychopathic or non-psychopathic?'

Hagan looks at her. 'Sorry?'

She smiles. 'That's the type of shite that we're supposed to be filling in on the crime scene report now. Bigwigs brought over this fella from fuckin Quantico, a fuckin FBI behavioural scientist.'

'Wow.' Hagan has no idea why Gallagher is sharing this information with him. But he knows that detectives never make idle conversation. If they are talking to you, it's because they think you are a potential suspect or a potential source of information.

'Yeah,' she goes on. 'How American is that? We had to sit through a four-hour fuckin lecture, and he hands us a' she breaks into a hoaky Southern American drawl 'What y'all call a memory stick. That's what we call a thumb drive. The study pack is loaded right on there for you guys.' She sounds like she's doing a turn in Gone With The Wind.

'Good accent,' Hagan lies.

She says, 'This looks personal. Did him so that he wouldn't have an open coffin.'

'Very personal,' he says. 'Do we have a confirmed ID then?'

She shakes her head, 'No. The dogs on the street are barking that it's Peter Fallon, but given the absence of a face and dental work, we'll have to let your lot do the fingerprints.'

Hagan begins to fill in the docket, Peter Fallon TBC. 'Who pronounced death?'

'Koomer?'

'Kumar.' Hagan writes that.

'Easiest three hundred quid he's ever going to earn,' she says.

Hagan asks, 'Are you the Garda on scene?'

'Fuck no. Fuck that. I'm not here. Put … em…' She scans the pub and sees a junior detective standing at the door, dutifully taking notes and examining the floor for some unknown reason. She calls out to him, 'Kiernan. Hey.'

Kiernan's head bolts upright like a meerkat in the zoo who's just spotted a kid firing a sweetie over the prison fence. 'Yes, Sergeant!'

'I'm nominating you as the on-scene here.'

'Thank you, Sergeant.'

She says to Hagan, 'Henry Kiernan.'

Hagan writes it into the docket, peels out a copy and hands it to her. 'I'll suit up.'

She smiles. 'Don't blame you. I'd wear one of those suits full-time if I was in your job. How's the new fella getting on?'

'Time will tell,' he says.

She shows him her phone, 'He's had his welcome post on Gangsta Rap.'

96

Hagan looks at the picture taken minutes ago of Joe sitting in the ambulance and staring out the window like a worried dog left in the carpark while its owner has gone shopping.

She says, 'Will he make it through the week?'

Hagan shrugs. 'Who knows if any of us will make it to the end of the week?'

For a moment, she stops. There was something in that, and she got it. She then covers it and says cheerfully, 'Can't argue with you there.' Her phone vibrates. She walks away and answers it, 'You want nice girl love you long time? ... Well, there was a definite pause there while you checked to see if you dialled the wrong number ... you wish, you fuckin pervert ... What's the craic, you bollox?'

Hagan kicks himself for showing his spurs as he makes his way to the ambulance and knocks on the passenger-side window. Joe looks up from his phone like he's got no idea where he is. Hagan points to the back of the ambulance. Joe gets out quickly and joins him in the rain at the back doors.

'Gloves,' Hagan says.

Joe roots in his pocket for a fresh pair of gloves, finds them, and puts them on.

'We're suiting up,' Hagan tells him as he opens the back of the ambulance, adjusts the hydraulic floor to raise the two bodies already in the back, and reveals another two stretcher bays underneath with two more gurneys. He then finds an extra large forensic suit and hands it to Joe. 'Take it slow and easy. Put it on one leg at a time.'

Hagan slips easily into his forensic suit.

The open doors of the ambulance offer some protection from the elements and privacy from the hoodies. Joe begins to put on the overalls well enough, first getting his feet into the plastic booties as if it was a giant baby-grow, pulling up the legs, but soon reaches the choke point. He cannot get his arms into the sleeves that dangle behind him. The task seems impossible; he verges on the edge of a panic attack. Hagan helps him by grabbing the collar and pulling it up to his neck, and, as if by magic, Joe is in the suit.

'Mask next.' Hagan hands him a fresh mask.

Joe fixes his face mask into place. It makes him feel a little hot and claustrophobic, but he sucks in a few lungfuls of the cold air, and it cools him down.

'Hood.'

Joe searches around behind his head for the hood. Can't find it. Hagan pulls it over his head for him and fixes the elasticated edges around the borders of his face. 'Always take the time to get the hood fixed properly. You don't want any blood or matter from the corpse getting into your hair or your ears. Yeah?'

Joe nods. He looks like a giant crime scene investigation baby.

Hagan asks him, 'What's next?'

Joe is blank.

'Goggles.'

Joe reaches into the back of the ambulance and pulls a fresh pair of goggles from the supply bag.

Hagan says, 'Never forget those goggles, you hear me?'

Joe nods, suited, masked and goggled up.

'You deal with the gurney, and I'll deal with the bodybags.'

Joe looks over at the hooded bad boys. *Take a picture now, losers.* He feels important as he wheels the gurney past the armed Gardai and into the inner sanctum of the crime scene.

Hagan stops at the entrance inside the pub, opens a heavy-duty bodybag, spreads it on the gurney, and then collapses it. Leaving the collapsed gurney at the entrance, he walks to the snug, taking the second bodybag with him. Joe follows him to the headless corpse, sitting calmly as if it is patiently waiting for them to come and collect it.

'Right,' Hagan says, 'We need to get the table out of here first.'

Joe nods.

Hagan keeps an eye on his rookie because you never can tell how a fella is going to respond to a mutilated body. He could turn and run, puke, faint, cry or crap himself. 'You okay?' he asks.

Joe makes a thumbs up.

'Let's get it done.' Hagan takes one end of the sticky, blood-covered table and waits. Joe grabs the other end but doesn't take his eyes off the corpse, watching it as if he expects it to stand up at any moment. 'Do you think his soul is still here?'

'No.'

'Where is it then?'

Hagan says, 'We're no different in death than we are in life. He's probably following the fella who killed him.'

'Like a ghost?'

'Like a ghost.'

'Haunting him?'

'Haunting him.'

'I heard that you don't have anything to fear from the dead.'

Hagan says, 'Whoever said that doesn't know much about the dead. Lift the table.'

Once the table has been peeled off the floor and moved out of the snug, Hagan says, 'This is going to get very messy very fast.'

Joe can't imagine how it can get any messier than it already is.

Hagan points at the floor. 'We'll open up the bodybag along here and lay the body into it. But once we lay it down, it's going to empty blood like we're pouring it out of a bucket. So the minute that we have it flat in the bag, you stand back. Yeah?'

Joe nods.

Tucking one end of the bodybag in under the feet of the sitting corpse, Hagan and Joe take a shoulder and arm each.

Hagan nods. 'Easy now, just let it go down onto its knees.'

It takes all their combined strength to move the large muscular torso out of the seat. The moment they move it, the gaping wound where the head used to be begins to gurgle and ooze blood like a pot of simmering spaghetti sauce. When they finally get the corpse onto its knees, Hagan says, 'Now just ease it down onto its belly.'

No sooner is the corpse flat, and Hagan's prediction is realised with buckets of blood. Joe remembers to step back while Hagan moves in and quickly zips up the bodybag. Loud gurgling sounds come from as it begins to fill up with fluids.

Hagan waits. 'Give it a minute or two to settle down.'

They stand for a moment in the empty pub.

The ceiling above them creaks.

Joe looks up and then looks at Hagan.

Hagan doesn't want to know who or what's walking around up there. A lot of murders have happened here in the Inn's two centuries, and a lot of dark souls have no place better to go to.

Joe whispers, 'Feels haunted.'

'You think?'

When the bag stops gurgling, they haul it to the collapsed gurney, place it into the clean bodybag, and zip it up. Voila! Everything is nice and tidy. The only evidence of the messy job is their protective suits.

'Let's peel off here,' Hagan says.

They remove the soiled plastic suits. Joe needs as much help getting out of his suit as he did getting into it. When they wheel the remains out to the ambulance, to the public eye, the body under cover on the gurney might have died peacefully over his pint while picking horses from the racing sheet. As Hagan gets the remains secured into the back of the ambulance, he notices Gallagher and her partner walking to him fast. They intercept a big fella in his thirties who has muscles on his muscles.

Gallagher puts her hand up to him. 'Hold it, Danny Boy.'

'I want to see him!'

Gallagher tells him, 'That's not possible.'

Danny Boy says, 'I just want to see his face!'

She says, 'That's not possible...'

He doesn't get it. 'What fuckin harm will it do?'

She says, 'He doesn't have a face,' and watches it register.

He steps back. 'So it's true what they're sayin?'

She makes the most false sympathetic smile she can manage and says, 'No head.'

He looks at her, knowing she is putting the boot into him. A rage builds in him that makes his neck glow red, and his veins protrude like an angry character in a cartoon. At the same time, a half dozen heavily armed gardai arrive around the scene. Ready to take him down hard if need be.

Danny Boy smiles at her and says, 'You know what, Gallagher? One day, you'll be found with no fuckin head too.'

Gallagher smiles at him. 'Is that a threat?'

'It's a prediction.' Then he turns and walks away.

Joe watches him go and says under his breath to Hagan, 'That was Danny Boy Delaney.'

Hagan says, 'Keep your mouth shut.'

Gallagher turns and smiles, but she's felt the chill of a death threat. 'Another unhappy customer.' She asks Hagan, 'You ready to go?'

'Ready.'

'We'll lead the escort.' She tells her subordinate officer, 'Have one of those armed units bring up the rear. Give them something to do instead of hanging around here like spare pricks at a wedding.'

Hagan and Joe get into the ambulance. Hagan says, 'Buckle up and hang on.'

No sooner has Joe buckled up, and they are lit up with the siren on and following Gallagher, who speeds out of the carpark like a bat out of hell. Hagan floors it all the way to keep up. Joe can't believe where the speedometer is – clocked out. Behind them, the sirens and lights flashing of two armed units follow them.

The Sunday morning convoy of four screaming sirens wakes up everyone in Ballyfermot, Chapelizod, Islandbridge, Stoneybatter, Smithfield, Phibsborough and Drumcondra as it makes its way across the city from the murder scene to the City Morgue.

# CHAPTER THIRTEEN

HAGAN WORKED ON the disembowelled washing machine in the middle of the kitchen floor as Val watched him from the table, drinking a cup of tea. 'It's amazing what's inside of a machine when you open it up like that.'

'It is.' He searched for a tool he knew he didn't have, but he was forming a plan. 'This carry-on of making screws that's neither a Phillips nor a flathead should be outlawed.'

She had no idea what that meant but nodded in agreement with him. 'Terrible.'

He worked at the odd-shaped screw-head with a self-tapping drill bit, trying to get a bite of it. 'This is all part of the plan to stop us from fixing things.' The self-tapping drill bit into the odd screw and worked to get it out of its housing. A small victory for DIY heads everywhere. 'There we go now.'

She adjusted the coaster on the table. 'Imagine if you weren't so handy with that kind of thing. We'd have to get a new one...'

He removed the motor from the machine's body like a delicate vital organ, 'There we go now,' wrapped it in an old towel and proudly showed it to her like a newborn. 'There it is now.'

'Amazing.' she sipped her tea. 'Just amazing.' She'd been secretly looking at a new machine in the Brilliant Bargains Super Store that everyone was talking about. But it was much too early to bring it up. There was a way to go before her husband threw in the towel on this old machine.

He ran his hand gently over the removed organ. 'I can have a look at the brushes now. You can see the discolouration. Look there.

That's a real tell-tale sign of overheating. I'll bet you anything that they're worn out.'

'It's not even that old,' she said, but she knew it was probably the oldest working washing machine in Dublin.

'Accelerated obsolescence.' He examined the old, worn-out motor. 'Putting weak materials into it and then not making spare parts. Odd screws and nuts and bolts. Making it impossible to fix. Forces you to buy a new one.'

'A new one?'

He shook his head. 'My mother had the same twin tub her whole married life. Had a mangle on it and everything. I used to love turning the sheets through it and the towels.'

'I remember that old twin tub with the mangle. You don't see them around any more.'

'They were great machines. My father bought it by the week.'

'Everything was by the week back then.' She tried to move him back into the present, back into getting a new washing machine. 'Things are cheaper now, thank God.'

'Made cheaper, but they end up being more expensive. People buy ten washing machines in a lifetime instead of one. And clothes? Don't even go there.'

'I know…' She was determined not to go there. Clothes will lead to a discussion about his father's George Webb shoes that he still has in the closet and wears on special occasions. That's half an hour down memory lane of shoe polishing and DIY cobbling. And God forbid that he looks at the watch he bought with his Holy Confirmation money when he was twelve, and it's still going. She bounces him back into the land of the new washing machine. 'We should have bought the extended warranty.'

'Not at all. That's another scam.'

'A scam, how?'

'They'll always find a way not to pay up. I've seen it countless times.'

'With washing machines?'

'With deaths. Life insurance.'

'What d'you mean?'

'They send the insurance investigators around to the house of the dead person to try and sniff out if the death was a suicide. They do be sitting in at the inquest and everything.'

'God. So you mean that they don't have to pay out if it's a suicide?'

'Nope. You have poor unfortunates who try to make it look like an accident so they can leave a few bob for the family. Next thing, the insurance investigators start digging into the medical history. If they find out that the deceased was told he had cancer or he was suffering any kind of illness that he didn't put on his policy – they have grounds not to pay out. Sometimes, they even turn up at the viewing or the funeral pretending to be old friends of the deceased and get talking to family members and friends. Someone says something in conversation like – he wasn't himself after he got fired. That's all they need to get wiggle room and start years of litigation with the widow.'

She looked around her. 'Everything is a scam these days,' she lost her appetite for the new washing machine and felt that this one, which they paid hard-earned money for, should still be working. 'I like this washing machine.'

'I know. But not to worry. I'm going to fix it. They can feck off if they think we're forking out for a new piece of crap.'

He made a habit of saying feck instead of fuck in the house. It meant the same thing but was an acceptable expletive to Val.

A whoosh of air caused by the dramatic opening of the front door came through the house, followed by an announcement, 'I'm home!' A second later, Molly was in the kitchen with a flushed face, a great flame of wild red hair and ready to explode with the good news.

Val asked, 'How did it go?'

'The Chase Agency want me!'

Val threw her arms in the air and wrapped her daughter in a big hug. 'Great news.'

He waited, wiping his hands with a rag.

Molly broke free of Val and hugged him. 'You need a shower, Dad.'

He liked to get smelly on his day off. He spent the rest of the week smelling like a disinfected corpse. It was a kind of therapy to remind himself what a living man smells like. That's the best shower, where he washed off the scent of natural sweat.

Val didn't mind the smell of sweat from her husband. She grew up in a world where men took a bath once a week. Her father would wash and shave every morning in cold water at the big Belfast sink in the outside toilet, smelling of carbolic soap when he went out to work in the morning. After a day of labouring on the docks, he would come home smelling of sweat, Guinness and Woodbine tobacco. She would sit on his lap and lie in his arms that were firm like a good leather chair, and she would fall asleep there in those wonderful smells that made her feel safe. It's the thing that she likes most about her husband: his hard body. There's no fat on him. There's no laziness in him. There's no lying in the bed in him. He does what it says on the tin: He's a man. She pats the chair next to her and says to Molly, 'Sit down and tell me all the details.'

Getting Molly to sit down was an almost impossible task. She was a being in constant motion through the universe, pacing the kitchen. 'I went into the Chase office. Dead fancy. Like, you wouldn't believe. And your one at the reception desk sticks her nose in the air and says to me, "Can I help you?" And I says, I'm here to see mister Chase. And she looks at me up and down and says, "Do you have an appointment?" And then she looks down her nose at her computer screen and says, "There's nothing in his diary." I'm just about to show her the text he sent me personally when the door to his office opens, and he tells her it's fine and brings me into his office. And the walls, all the walls, are covered with pictures of like everyone who's anyone, like big-time. Dennis Doyle is one of his clients.

Val nodded 'Dennis Doyle. That's amazing.'

Molly takes a breath and continues, 'And I'm like, I can't believe he represents all of these really famous people, and I'm like here. He tells me to take a seat and asks me if I want a tea or a coffee or water or coke. I'm like, coke, please. Then he presses the button on something on his desk and tells the snotty one at the reception to bring in two cokes with ice and lemon. Ha. So right away, he says, "Look – I'm not going to beat around the bush here. I saw your showreel, and you've got Jazz and tap on your CV and singing, right?" I just nod, delighted he's asking about the skills that I actually do have, and in the back of my mind, I'm praying, please don't ask about the horse riding and the fencing because I don't have a clue. But he says to me, "I think you're a fit for a very nice supporting role that Marcus Strauss has been trying to cast. He's looking for a young Maureen O'Hara."'

Val held up her hand like she had a message from Jesus for the church, 'Marcus Strauss – Oh my God!'

Molly mirrored her mother. 'I know. I'm like, no way. No way. Marcus Strauss. Maureen O'Hara! Are you joking me? Of course, I don't say that to him. Then the door opens, and the snotty one comes in with two glasses of coke with ice and lemon on a tray and puts it on the little coffee table, and then I make a point of saying a big thank you that's really a fuck you, and she can't even look at me, and she sneaks back out. I say to him, Mister Chase - and he says, "I'm gonna stop you right there, Molly. Call me Jeff," he says, "Mister Chase is my father." And then he says, "Tell me a little bit about yourself. What's your story?" So, off I go tellings him about me, you know, how I started out being the Jam Tart Princess and then Annie, and he shakes his head and says, "I gotta stop you. I saw that production of Annie. You were great." Great, that's what he said. Anyway! Long story short. He's setting up a meeting for me with Marcus Strauss. I can't believe it. Look at me. What the am I like?' Molly stopped for breath and water.

Val said quickly in the gap, 'That's great.'

Molly held her hands up wide like an evangelist preacher hitting the money slot in a biblical story, 'I think this is it!'

Given their history with the old agent, Lady Linda, Val was careful of agents. She asked, 'Did he talk about a contract?'

'Of course. He said they'll cover all that after I meet with the producer. And you'll never guess what else he said.'

Val held her smile, already suspicious of the lack of detail on the contract. 'What?'

Molly looked at Hagan. 'Dad?'

He was lost. 'What?'

Molly pointed her finger at her father. 'He said what you said.'

'What I said?'

'Yes.'

Val asked him, 'What did you say?'

'I don't know.' He looked at Molly. 'What did I say?'

Molly put her hands on her head to contain a revelation that might explode. 'He said he knows talent when he sees it!'

'Did I say that?'

'You said it the other day – you said that I have it. That I was born with it.'

He looked to Val, who was already wounded. This was not good ground for him; he was out of his lane and standing on Val's turf. He immediately began an evasive manoeuvre. 'Well, I said it, but your Mam is always saying it.'

Val patted the table as if she were seconding a proposal at a union meeting. 'I've been saying that since you were four years old.'

'I know,' Molly held her hand up in a mea culpa pose. 'I know. Sorry.' Then turned back to her freight train of information. 'Anyway. I'm going to meet Marcus Strauss tomorrow. For lunch. Lunch! Apparently, the film is already in preproduction, and they're desperate to cast the part. They've seen every redhead in the world already, so it's not like it will be one of those cattle call casting sessions where I'm sitting in the waiting room with twenty other redheads, and we're all mumbling the same lines for the audition. It's lunch!'

'That's great,' Val said and looked at Hagan.

'Wonderful,' Hagan said and looked at Val, who was letting him know it was up to him to say what they were both thinking. He said, 'Just don't sign anything until we've had a chance to have someone look at it.'

Molly shook her head. 'I'm not stupid.'

He didn't follow it on. He knew he'd let enough air out of her balloon. He just nodded and smiled, and looked at his work.

Molly suddenly noticed the washing machine. 'What happened?'

Val said, 'It died.'

Molly said, 'It was making that weird noise. Did it blow up?'

'No. I took it apart.'

'Why?'

'I'm fixing it.'

Molly laughed. 'The Doctor Frankenstein of dead appliances. They're going to start moving around the house on their own.' She disappeared out the door. 'I need a shower.'

Hagan and Val shared a look that can transfer twenty years of history in microseconds.

# CHAPTER FOURTEEN

YOU'RE ALWAYS GUARANTEED a grant Guinness in Flanagan's of Dalkey, where the cosy labyrinthine layout makes for a perfect watering hole, serving the needs of drinking cohorts, as well as the lone wolves who prefer to sit at the bar and watch the herd from over the rim of a pint glass. Hagan has situated himself on a high stool at the east end of the long bar from where he can get a good view of the three men who are his quarry: Jeffery Chase, who's sitting in a corner, smiling and listening to DJ Dennis who's telling an amazing story about an amazing escapade he was on with his producer friend Marcus Strauss whose eyes never stop scanning the room in a perpetual state of unease like a junkie whose skin is itching from the inside out. Hagan's going to kill Marcus Strauss tomorrow. Then, the day after tomorrow, he's going to kill DJ Dennis Doyle, but tonight, all going well, he's going to kill Jeffery Chase. He must kill all three in quick succession before they figure out he's coming for them.

Around the three soon-to-be-dead-bastards sits a cohort of sycophants, force-glued into the stupid story and waiting for a gap to laugh as loud as they can, each laughing louder than the other so that you'd think Bob Hope was doing the jokes. Of course, DJ Dennis has no idea who's listening to him, nor does he care, much like when he's doing his radio show on a cocaine-fuelled yappaton. High on the sound of his own voice, he speaks quicker than he can breathe until he hits the punchline and comes to an abrupt stop, inhaling hard, nodding, holding up his hands, and offering a punctuation point for the cohort to show their appreciation. They clap and laugh, and one of them starts choking on how deadly funny the story is.

Hagan savours a mouthful of his pint, lingering in the moment of the malt-sweetness turning to hop-bitterness as it runs over his tongue and hits the back of his throat. Some things take time and precision and he's a man built of patience with a seagull's eyes for detail. He's surveilled the three fuckers, and been meticulous in recording their behavioural patterns over a few weeks. They are not extraordinary. They live to an unconscious behavioural algorithm just like every other creature on the planet. Each gets up, goes to work, and comes home. They party on the weekends, and Sunday is their pints and cocaine procession when they spend the day being driven around various watering holes by DJ Dennis's driver. The ritual always ends in Flanagan's because all three men live in Dalkey.

While their murders have by now been meticulously planned, there are elements beyond Hagan's control. Earlier in the day, for instance, the murder of the talent agent Jeffery Chase was not set in stone because Hagan needed a helping hand from Mother Nature. The location where he plans to kill the fucker is overlooked, and he needs cover. Thankfully, by teatime, the forecasted sea fog rolled into the bay, pushed up against Killiney Hill, and came to a halt, covering the coastal village of Dalkey in a blanket. It was only then that He knew for sure that tonight was the night. Now he watches DJ Dennis tap his nose and wink at Marcus Strauss. Jeffery Chase waves a finger at the barman to settle the tab like he's conducting an orchestra. Hagan knows all of these cues and finishes the final quarter of his pint in a long, satisfying swallow and feels the warm glow in his gut as he sets the empty glass back on the counter; the remains of the creamy head cling to the inside of the glass, bearing witness to what a grand pint it was. He nods thanks to the barman and eases his way through the chatting locals. He's a man who knows how to be invisible on crime scenes as he goes about his business of tagging and bagging corpses. He passes through the self-obsessed living like a ghost into the night.

Outside the pub, cold, wet air wipes his face, and salty sea fog burns his eyes a little as he peers into the dark and makes out the parking lights of DJ Dennis's chauffeured black Mercedes, barely visible, even though it is parked only twenty yards from the pub's doors. What needs to happen next is simple. DJ Dennis has a house on the Killiney Hill just off the Vico road. Marcus Strauss has a place on the same road. Jeffery Chase lives in an apartment overlooking Coliemore Harbour. DJ Dennis will drop Chase off on his way home and present Hagan with the perfect opportunity to make the kill. But Hagan needs to get to Coliemore Harbour before they do so he can set up, and he's got a plan for that.

Using Molly's e-scooter, he takes off into the fog. The sharp taste of salt on his lips is a wonderful contrast to the Guinness. It feels like he's travelling a hundred miles an hour through the cloud, and he reminds himself, *don't get giddy on all the adrenalin that's pumping through you now – this is the time when mistakes can be made.* Turning hard left at a shortcut up Rockfort Avenue, he comes to what appears to be a dead end, but he discovered, during his planning, a small tight lane wide enough only for one person that cuts between two houses. He goes through it fast; it spits him out onto the hill, where the road quickly drops, and he picks up more speed. If he hits anything, he'll be banjaxed. Still, he doesn't let up, riding on the razor edge of control, keeping his nerve, leaning hard to the right and continuing fast downhill on Colimore Road until he comes to the harbour, where he stops and listens to the unseen waves crashing at the walls and making the ground shudder. High tide was an hour ago. Somewhere in the black, small boats strain to hold onto their moorings, creaking and moaning as the retreating tide tries to pull them away to the open sea. His back starts acting up. He'll need to do some heavy lifting and he can't have it pack in on him. Taking a card of pills from his pocket, he weighs up the duel demand of killing the pain and keeping a sharp mind and decides that one pill should be enough to make it bearable and stay sharp enough to get the job done.

He's studied every inch of this small ancient harbour: the jagged tripping points, the mossy slipway, the walkway to the harbour's mouth, and a nook in the wall that makes a blindspot from the road and gives him a view of the entrance gates to the apartment complex; where he now waits, watching his watch and worrying that they might not come, that they might have made a change of plan. Cold sets into his bones. His primordial failure to protect his child closes its mouth around him and threatens to swallow him, but his heart is lifted by the faint glow of headlights emerging from the fog. He's filled with the pure primitive instinct for retribution that has propelled his genetic line for the last three hundred thousand years; everything in him quickens as the black car slides into view and eases to a stop. The back door opens, and Jeffery Chase rolls out, laughing. Thankfully, DJ Dennis doesn't have his driver wait until Chase gets through the iron gates into the safety of the walled apartment complex. The car pulls away and disappears into the night. Chase stands in the darkness for a moment, getting his bearings. Hagan needs to intercept his prey before it opens the gate and activates the floodlights that will illuminate the area for the security cameras. He moves in fast, coming behind it and applying a necklock. It bucks, but there's no strength in the fucker. There's something repulsive about the struggling gelly fat. He holds the wriggling jelly bag in the neck lock until it scutters itself and goes limp, then he puts it on his shoulder and carries it through the covered walkway to the harbour's mouth that presents a dark gap into the fast-flowing deadly waters of Dalkey Sound.

The investigation of a sudden and unexpected death is a puzzle in three parts: cause, mechanism and manner of death. Hagan needs this shitbag to be breathing and making a real effort for life when it goes into the water so that the subsequent post-mortem examination will show that the mechanism of death was hypoxemia and irreversible cerebral anoxia, with water deep in his airways to show that it was alive when it went into the sea. This presentation will give enough solid forensics to prove the cause of death to be drowning. With no bruises on the corpse and toxicology showing that it is full of alcohol and narcotics, it will ease through the post-mortem examination, and the manner of death will be found to be an accident or a suicide.

Hagan fucks the shitbag over the wall and hears the loud, satisfying splash and gulp of the sea swallowing it whole into the fast-flowing abyss. The night tightens around him; some part of himself is snagged to the shitbag, like a fish struggling on a line. Then it is gone. Snapped. He's free of it and filled with exhilaration as every atom in his body rejoices in the victory of having annihilated one of his child's killers. He gets it under control because he is far from done, and he has no right to be happy. Carefully making his way back along the walkway, using the harbour wall as a guide, he reaches the road again, finds Molly's e-scooter where he left it, and takes off into the night. Zipping along in the darkness, he remembers the Christmas morning when Molly unwrapped the scooter, and they brought it out onto the road and took turns whizzing up and down on it. Even Val came out and had a go.

# CHAPTER FIFTEEN

MOLLY BOUNCED AROUND the living room like a moth caught in a lampshade. 'Is the car outside?'

Val looked on, worried that her daughter might get too excited. She always got herself into this state before an audition. The only casting she wasn't nervous about was her first one for Annie. Val was also calm and collected then because they didn't know the ramifications of getting the part. Having lived through the era of fame in Annie, they were both very much aware of what it meant for Molly to get a good part in a major motion picture now that she was trying to make the move up from being a child actor. This part was a proper career starter. But this was more than an audition; it was a screen test, and in the world of casting, it meant that, unless Molly did something catastrophic, she was about to be cast into the role. The single worst catastrophe that can occur in a screen test is sweating.

'Breathe,' Val said.

'I'm breathing. I'm breathing. In out. In out. How do I look?'

Val knows that there's no point lying to her. If she doesn't compose herself, she'll blow it. 'Hot and flustered.'

Molly stops still, closes her eyes, feels her body's weight on the soles of her feet, and grounds herself. When she was taught the technique in drama school, she thought it was silly. But of course, like all the skills and techniques she was learning there, it was theory to be put into practice because you cannot recreate the atmosphere of the real thing in a classroom. Sure, you might get some butterflies doing your monologue in front of your peers, but that is a world away from standing in front of an audience, a casting agent, or a director and putting all on the line. But Molly isn't all that worried about her nerves because she knows that the moment she steps in front of an audience, the jitters will leave her, and she will feel wholly centred on the stage. Performance for her is comforting, familiar, and part of her childhood. Her ability to rise to a new level under pressure proves her to be the real deal. At least, that's how it is when she steps onto the stage. But she's never stepped in front of a camera before.

Hagan enters the room and hits the brakes. 'You look amazing. A million dollars.'

'Thank you,' Molly says.

Val asks her, 'Have you got your lines?'

'Yes.'

Val looks around. 'Where are they?'

Molly taps her head. 'Memorised.'

Val looks worried. 'Are you sure? Do you want to run them with me?'

Molly becomes still, like standing water; everything, even the air around her, stops. She can lay down a beat like a silent tonne of air before a line. 'No. Thank you.' She stays still, her eyes closed. Her parents know that she's running those lines in her head. And both of them know that she has the lines perfectly memorised.

Molly's phone pings and she reads it. 'The car is here.'

'Break a leg,' Val says.

Hagan smiles and nods. He knows he can't say good luck, and he doesn't like the term, break a leg. He stands with Val at the front window, watching Molly leave the house and walk to the black S-Class Mercedes the producer sent to bring her to the studio for her screen test.

As Molly nears the car, the groomed and suited driver says, 'Good morning, Miss Hagan,' and opens the back for her.

'Thank you,' she says, entering the dark interior shrouded in privacy glass. The doors close, and she is sealed into a cocoon of privilege. As the car glides along the road, she sees people stopping to look, but she knows they cannot see the VIP in the back seat; she feels like a movie star. There's an old saying in the theatre business: "Don't start thinking about the dressing room wallpaper before you get the part". But Molly didn't care to keep her imagination in check; even if she wanted to, she couldn't. By the time they reached the studio gates she was putting the final touches to her Oscar acceptance speech.

'We've arrived,' the driver told her as the red and white striped barrier raised; the security guard smiled and waved, and the car eased along the narrow tree-lined path to the studio complex.

The driver asked, 'Would you like the air conditioning turned up?'

'Sorry?'

He explained, 'To cool the interior?'

She realised that she was sweating. 'Yes, please.'

Cold air circulated inside the car. A moment later, they came to a halt. A young, plain woman wearing jeans, a t-shirt, an earpiece, and hugging a clipboard to her bosom opened the door and said into the walkie-talkie, 'She's arrived.' Then she smiled at Molly and said, 'Miss Hagan, Welcome. I'm Anna, one of the ADs. If you can come with me to costume, hair and make-up?'

Molly smiled, got out, and looked around to thank the driver, but he stayed in the car. So she followed Anna, who was walking at a pace like they were already late and spoke in a low frantic voice into her walkie-talkie, 'We're walking now.'

The wardrobe department was hot and fussy. The wardrobe mistress looked over Molly with a trained eye and disappeared into a wrack of costumes and reappeared holding a green skirt and jacket while at the same time, an assistant appeared with a matching blouse and held them up to Molly. The mistress smiled, 'Lovely. Do you want to pop that on?' And she motioned to a curtained area. Anna stood on the opposite side of the curtain, nervously tapping the clipboard while Molly dressed into the costume. It felt tight. When she came out the mistress looked and nodded. 'Lovely'

Anna perked up. 'Great. Hair and Makeup are ready.'

'Don't forget the shoes!' The wardrobe assistant popped a pair of heels in front of Molly, and she stepped into them. She didn't like them or the outfit, but she didn't say. As she followed the trainer-shod Anna, she did her best to keep up without breaking an ankle, recalling a golden rule that she had ignored: "Don't wear a costume you're not comfortable in, even if your character is supposed to be uncomfortable."

Hair and makeup got to work. The chat was kept to a minimum. Anna stood in the corner, tapping her clipboard, while Molly was transformed into a World War Two pinup girl. They struggled with her hair but got it under control and stood back with their hands out. Done. Off she set again after the human greyhound Anna. The corridor to the sound stage was empty as Anna brought her along, again updating the walkie-talkie on their progress to a door with a sign that read, DO NOT ENTER WHEN RED LIGHT IS ON. The red light over the door was on, so they waited. Anna drummed her tight, clipped nails on her clipboard.

A buzzer buzzed somewhere, a bell rang, and the light changed to green. Anna opened the door and entered first. 'Mind your step.'

Molly's eyes adjusted to the darkness in time to see the power cables running like snakes across the floor. Ahead of her, she made out a solitary chair illuminated in a dark space. What was in the darkness she could not see but imagined it was a set; then she made out a group of people gathered around the pool of light, sitting in chairs and scribbling their thoughts about the actor who had just screen-tested. The young man made his way out and winked at her as he passed. It wasn't until he had vanished into the darkness that she realised he was a star. Her heart skipped a beat.

Anna started talking into the dark, 'This is Molly Hagan, testing for the young Scarlett O'Hara.'

Murmurs rippled in the dark, and the Director emerged, purposefully messy-haired and designer-shaggy, like a caricature of the corporate creative department. 'Hello again, Molly.'

She shook his hand. She'd read for him twice. He made her uneasy because he never made eye contact with her. Maybe that was part of his act, she thought.

'You have the sides?' he asked.

Molly tapped her head, 'All in here.'

He paused momentarily as if examining her answer and then laughed a little. 'Very good.'

Another young woman, maybe an assistant to the director, gestured to Molly. 'Would you like to take the seat?'

Molly walked to the chair in the centre of the light pool. In her peripherals, she watched the group of people. The Producer was there, talking into another man's ear. That man wore a suit and nodded. She sat in the chair and could see nothing but the light.

*Don't squint*, she told herself. The skirt felt tight. *Don't fidget*. She took a breath and tried to relax. Then, the lens of the camera came into view.

The Director's voice spoke from the dark. 'Checks?'

The pair of hair and makeup women darted from the dark and began to tag team on her, one trying to get control of the wild hair that was breaking out of its binds, and the other patting down her face with more makeup, and she knew why: She was seating...

The checks vanished quickly into the darkness, and she was alone again in the light.

The clapperloader appeared with the clapperboard and held it up in front of Molly's face. A voice from the dark said, 'Molly Hagan. Testing for Scarlet.'

Another voice from the dark said, 'And we're rolling.'

The clapper snapped shut and disappeared.

'We'll go for a take,' the Director said. 'Just natural, Molly, like you did for the audition. In your own time. And action.'

Molly heard herself say the lines that sounded alien and flat, like someone else was reading them aloud with no character. All the time, she felt a trickle of sweat roll down her forehead, along the edge of her eyebrow and then into her eye, where it burned, but she dared not wipe it. When she reached the end of the monologue, the Director said, 'And cut.'

She waited. There was a flurry of discussion in the dark. Someone said, 'Do we need to go again?' and someone else said, 'I think we're good.' Then the Director said, 'Thank you, Molly.'

The assistant emerged saying, 'This way,' and gestured into the darkness.

Molly heard herself saying 'Thank you,' but couldn't be sure if the words came out. No one else spoke to her much as she followed Anna through the building, back to the costume department, undressed and dressed again in her clothes, and removed the makeup. Eventually, Anna brought her back to the car she came in, and the driver opened the door; she got in, the door closed, and she was unceremoniously driven out of the studio. She was glad that people could not see into the back seat as they moved through the city traffic; she was sure she looked as miserable as she felt. She'd have to put on some kind of a face for her mother and father, and she didn't want the limousine pulling up outside of her house for all the neighbours to see, all waiting on the big news.

'Can you pull over?'

The driver brought the car to a stop. She wasn't sure where she'd asked him to stop. 'I'll make my own way from here. Thank you.'

She got out, he drove on, she started walking through the crowds, and soon felt anonymous, just another one of the millions going about their lives, all with their own problems. On the bus home, she composed what she would tell her parents; she wouldn't say she blew it, she'd say that she didn't know how it went, she'd have to wait and see, and then she would let a week or so pass before saying she didn't get the part. She rehearsed it as she came into the kitchen but just burst into tears when she saw them and was immediately hugged by her mother and then her father.

# CHAPTER SIXTEEN

HAGAN NAVIGATES THE ambulance along the Vico Road, snaking through the darkness up the side of Killiney Hill. The twinkling necklace of the city's coastal lights hangs around the horseshoe bay. At regular intervals, the northside of the black bay's waters are stroked by a wand of light from the southside lighthouse.

Joe wipes the salty condensation from the passenger side window, looks into the warped darkness, and makes out the head of Howth sketched against the grey pre-dawn on the horizon. 'Howth looks weird from over here.'

'Weird?' Hagan carefully follows the track of his headlights along the black tar road that disappears for heart-stopping moments and reappears in a deadly game of peekaboo on the cliff edge.

'I've never seen it from this side.' Joe says and thinks about his new perspective. 'What do you think it is?'

'What what is?'

'The body.'

'Killiney Beach. Probably a swimmer.'

Hagan is sure they're picking up the body of Jeffery Chase and wonders how long it will be before they find the body of Harry Murphy, and when they do, how long will it be before Detective Gallagher links it to the death of Jeffery Chase? He's sure she will join the dots when Marcus Strauss and Dennis Doyle turn up dead. Then she will come for him.

Joe says, 'Don't know how they swim in that cold water.'

'It's very good for you.'

'Do you do it?'

'I try to get in a few times a week.'

'Where?'

'Dollymount.'

'What does it feel like?'

'The first time you do it, it seems unbearable. Your body is hit with a cold shock. But if you stick it out and go through the pain, a wonderful sensation fills you. Almost like you're on fire.'

'Fire? I don't think I'd like that.'

'Good fire.'

Joe rolls his lips like he's sucking on what he wants to say and turns the words into a chewed-up, 'Hmm.'

'The health benefits are well recorded.'

'Maybe someone jumped in, you know, like a suicide?' Joe says.

'That's also a possibility. Or they could have been walking along the cliffs and slipped.'

'Or fell off a boat,' Joe says. 'I'd say that happens a lot. People falling off boats.'

'I'd say.'

'When I was on the big cruise ship with me ma and me nanna, I was looking over the edge and thinking if I fell in there, I'd be a gonner. Made me dizzy looking at it. Like I could fall in from being dizzy.'

'Happens a lot at cliff edges.'

'Yeah?'

'People rush to the edge of the cliff to get the great view and then find out that they have vertigo. Over they go.'

'I don't like cliffs. Or things that spin you around, you know, like the rides they have in amusement parks?'

'Can't say I'm fond of any of that meself.'

'One time on a roller coaster, I vomited, and all the people behind me got covered in it.'

'Yeah?'

'Did you ever pick up someone who fell off a boat?'

'No.'

Hagan cuts the cut down Strathmore Road. The tall flanking trees form a tunnel to block out any light the moon might offer, making it pitch dark as the road descends like the entrance to the underworld.

'How many bodies have you picked up from the sea?'

'Lots. Most of them from here.'

'Here?'

'Killiney Bay is the natural wash-up point for a body that went into the water anywhere along the south side of the bay. If a body goes into the water on the northside, it's likely to be taken out of the bay to the open sea.'

'Right,' says Joe, rolling the theory around in his head like a handful of marbles, testing it until a new question pops up. 'What if a body goes into the Liffey? Like that's in the middle.'

'If the tide is coming in, it's going to end up at the weir up at Huston Station. If the tide is going out, it runs a fifty-fifty chance of getting pulled into either the north or south side currents, but it also runs the risk of being annihilated by propeller blades in the busy shipping lanes there.'

Joe nods with knowledge on the subject. 'I've seen those propellers. There was a video of them when I got a tour of the engine room on the cruise ship. They're as big as a house.'

Hagan examines the darkness beyond the headlight beams. 'I know the turn is somewhere along here… Practically blind here.'

Joe watches the grey carpet of clouds that floats around them. 'You'd think we were in the Amazon or something. That's weird-looking fog. Covering up the road.'

'It's not fog. It's dew.'

'What's the difference?'

'Fog comes from the sky. Dew comes from the ground.'

Hagan slows to a crawl and puts on his rolling safety lights that form a light dome. A hypnotised fox stands in front of them, trapped in amazement by the swirling light show. Hagan flashes his high beams to break the spell. The fox disappears. Further along, what he's looking for comes into view – the tight dogleg of a cut that makes a narrow lane from the road to the beach. Carefully, he negotiates his way down it. 'Let's hope the body is not too far from the car park.'

The entrance to the secluded beach carpark is made under a low railway bridge that was put in place two hundred years ago. The narrow stone walls glisten like the scales of a giant reptile until the tight arch gives way to the great expanse of beach running five miles along the coast to Bray Head. Immediately ahead, a square of sand and gravel creates a corral big enough to accommodate a dozen cars at a door-scraping squeeze. To his right, a uniformed garda stands in a natural nook that's formed in the stone-made rail embankment, taking what cover she can find from the weather that's swirling violently, trying to find a way to get at her. Seaspray caught in the wind shoots around the rocks like a demented cat after a mouse. The point-duty garda breaks her cover and endures the wrath of the elements to open the crime scene tape and let the morgue ambulance through.

Joe leans forward in his seat, suddenly fascinated. 'Wow. Two technical bureau vans, three squad cars and a detective car. It must be a murder?'

'We'll find out.'

Hagan worries that his presentation of Jeffery hasn't worked. Do they think that there's something suspicious about the death?

Roughly three hundred yards along the beach, they can see the glowing halo in the fog from the work lights inside a white forensic tent that is taking a battering from the elements but holding its ground like a determined storm lantern. The silhouettes of the technical team working inside it slide along its white plastic walls.

Joe says, 'It looks like a puppet show.'

'What kind of puppet shows did you watch?'

'In Bali.'

'You were in Bali?'

'With me Ma and me Nana. We did a cruise there. It was on Nana's bucket list.'

'Okay. Wow. You're a man of the world.'

Hagan's lights illuminate a half dozen detectives clustered in conversation around one of the cars as he reverses the ambulance into a spot between the two technical bureau vans. No sooner has he parked the ambulance when Gallagher makes her way to his window.

'Lovely morning for it,' she says and peers at Hagan from under her hood. Her eyes are always bright and inquisitive, but Hagan can see a shade of worry in them.

'Detective Gallagher.' He acts surprised to see her here. He knows why she's attending this particular scene, and he shows no interest in the crime scene apart from the information he needs to remove the body. 'We're in the tent?'

She nods. 'There's nothing suspicious on it. We put the tent up because, you know, paparazzi have already gotten wind of the fact that the dead fella is a VIP.'

Hagan fills with a secret relief to hear that it's nothing suspicious, and worries that his joy might flash to the honed senses of Gallagher like a sprat catching the eye of a mackerel. But she has other things on her mind. She knows that the dead VIP is a customer of one of her informers, who is a drug dealer. She's been trying to call the informer, but he's not picking up. Hagan busies himself in his routine, taking out his morgue docketbook with the pen ready to fill it in. 'He's been identified then?'

'No. Not officially.'

Hagan nods. 'We should get on with it then. The weather is only going to get worse.'

Gallagher nods and darts back to the detective cluster. Hagan and Joe exit the ambulance, put on their long black rubber raincoats and walk to the back doors to retrieve a body bag and the stretcher.

'Gloves.' Hagan says to Joe.

'Sorry,' Joe says and fumbles in his pocket. 'Don't know why I keep forgetting.'

'You're not forgetting.'

'But–'

'You're just not remembering.'

Joe is lost. 'Is that not the same thing?'

'No. You're relying on a habit that you haven't formed yet. You've remembered to put them in your pocket because you know you're going to forget them. You're giving yourself a licence not to remember them. Don't carry a pair in your pocket any more. Get into the habit of grabbing a pair from the box on the dashboard and putting them on before you get out of the ambulance.'

Joe keeps any protest he might have to himself and nods in compliance.

The pair of bodymen labour through the foggy dew over the uneven terrain of large round stones that get smaller as they near the waterline until underfoot turns into soft boot-sucking sand.

Joe licks his lips. 'Salty.'

'It's good for you.'

Somewhere in the dark the waves are breaking and crashing and sending sea spray into the air. They come to the glowing white tent as a garda from the technical bureau comes out in his white forensic suit, holding his hood in place on his head from the elements. 'All yours.'

When they enter the tent, Joe recognises the corpse. 'Jeffery Chase.'

'You know him?'

'I know who he is.'

'Who is he?'

'He's one of the judges on the talent show – you know – A Star Is Born. On the telly.'

'I don't watch the telly.'

Joe laughs, then stops. 'Really?'

'Really.'

Joe nods. 'Anyway. He's the kind one because he's a talent agent and takes the winner onto his books. DJ Dennis is on the show as well. He's the funny one, and then Marcus Strauss, who is a producer, is the one who is grumpy and points out the contestant's faults. All of the talent shows have the same three, you know, the grumpy one, the funny one and the kind one.'

'Well. Thanks for filling me in.' Hagan writes John Doe on the ID bracelet.

Joe is confused. 'Why are we bringing him in as a John Doe?'

Hagan could explain to his rookie that the PR machine is already preparing for the fallout that will occur when the toxicology report confirms Jeffery Chase's blood was loaded with cocaine at the time of his death. Then, DJ Dennis and Marcus Strauss will make a combined touching testimony to their troubled friend who struggled secretly with addiction. ( It was so secret that Jeffery didn't do drugs in front of his VIP friends.) A speechwriter will compose a dewy sentence or two about how we can never really know what is going on with someone and how we shouldn't be afraid to reach out and ask for help. (Making the backhanded point that Jeffery never asked any of his VIP friends for help.) There will then be a few more trenches of good spin doctor work between now and the outcome of the Coroner's findings to put space between Jeffery Chase and his co-hosts on the high-rating TV talent show. By the time the Coroner's findings are released, Jeffery Chase will have been transformed from a much-loved TV personality to a lonely, secretive drug addict with no mates. So, to answer Joe's question, even though everyone on the beach knows the corpse's identity, no one wants to get tied to the toxic fallout by being the person who makes the formal identification.

Hagan says, 'Just procedure for now.'

Joe nods. 'Where's his trousers?'

'The current takes them. Surprised he's not completely naked.' Hagan kneels and puts the ID bracelet on the fat wrist. He expected that he might get some sense of a belligerent presence here around the body, angry at Hagan for having committed the murder. But there is nothing here. He doesn't know what fate awaits Jeffery in the next life with the ancients, but he knows they took his soul to some terrible place, and he hopes the cunt suffers there for eternity.

Joe opens out the bodybag and places it on the stretcher, ready to receive the corpse.

'So if he wasn't murdered, why have they got all these detectives here and the tent and the forensics and all?'

'You were right.'

'About what?'

'It's a puppet show.'

'I'm not following you.'

'He's a VIP. There will be a media frenzy. They're pouring on the gravy to make sure their arses are covered. The superintendent can stand before the cameras and say, we did everything we could – there's no stone left unturned.'

'Right. I get it now.' Joe shakes his head at the skullduggery of it all.

'Speaking of stones unturned, be very careful carrying the stretcher out there. The ground is lethal. And he's a big fella and bloated.'

'Right.' Joe looks at the enlarged drum-tight blue belly. It reminds him of one of those gender reveals that everyone is doing now, where they burst a giant balloon, and pink or blue confetti explodes from it, depending on the sex of the unborn baby. 'Why is he bloated like that?'

'Gas. You start to decompose from the inside out. The stomach and intestines start first. Makes sense, right? They're full of bacteria for digesting food. That body is just as much alive now as it was when it was walking around. But alive with bacteria rapidly liquifying the internal organs and fermenting the juices, creating a lot of gas. Amazing when you think about it. But the problem for us is that the gas gets trapped in there.'

'Me Nanna used to get that trapped gas thing.'

'Yeah?'

'We used to have to give her a tablet to make her fart.'

'Right.'

'It was a powerful smell.'

'I'd say.'

Hagan watches Joe think about his nana's farts for a moment and then interrupts his memories. 'God be good to her.'

Joe nods in agreement. 'I don't really believe in God.'

'That's okay,' Hagan says.

'Do you?'

'If you're asking me, do I believe that there is an all-powerful being who made us in his image and then decided to add in childhood cancer for the craic? No, I don't believe that.'

'Right. So you don't believe in a life after death.'

'I didn't say that.' Hagan gestures to the waiting corpse. 'Are you ready for the lift now?'

'Yeah. Sorry. I don't mean to ask so many questions.'

'That's okay. There's about sixteen stone in him, so get a good grip, straight back, bend the knees, lift with the legs.'

'Got it.' Joe squats, grabs the ankles and waits for the count. Hagan takes the wrists. Joe thinks about the people on the beach looking at the tent and watching the shadow puppet show of two bodymen lifting a bloated corpse.

'One more thing,' Hagan says. 'When we lift the corpse, some of that gas will find a way out. There are only two orifices, and we have one of each. So be ready for an enormous fart.'

'Okay…'

Hagan counts, 'One - Two.'

They lift the body and trigger an explosive corpse fart that sings out like an opera tenor holding an impossibly long and high note; the heady concoction of active hydrogen sulphide and methane fills the tent with an eye-scorching trachea-cauterising gas cloud. They quickly place the volatile gas-bomb-corpse in the bodybag as green and yellow slime of putrefaction starts to ooze from the mouth like puss from a lanced boil.

Hagan quickly zips on the bodybag. 'Straps.'

Joe's lungs try to close like two fists inside his chest, fighting against the air he is forcing into them as he tightens the lower straps of the stretcher. Hagen fastens the torso and shoulder straps and says, 'This will be like carrying a sixteen-stone bag of water. The corpse is going to move around a lot on the stretcher. So we need these straps to be tight.' A loud gurgling growl from the corpse answers the tug of the strap over the torso. Once the body is secured, Hagan goes to the head and Joe to the feet.

Hagan counts, 'one – two – lift.'

They lift the stretcher and get out of the stinking tent.

Outside, the much-welcomed cold, wet wind washes their faces in sea spray.

'Let's just take a moment here and breathe. Clean out the lungs,' Hagan says.

They face into the wind and suck in lungfuls of the purifying air.

After a few moments, Hagan says, 'Let's go. Carefully. Don't take a step until your standing foot is firmly down. Take your time.'

Joe feels his ankle give a warning twitch as he steps awkwardly on the uneven stones that slide away underfoot, never sure when his boot will stop sinking and find a grip. They work their way up the slope of the beach from low water to high ground, careful step by careful step. One step sends all the weight to Joe; the next sends it back to Hagan. It's torture on the ankles and knees and quads and calves and glutes. If they were men of leisure and spent their time in a gym playing at doing manual labour with weights in front of a big mirror, they'd call this a leg day and high-five each other.

A series of quick-fire white flashes momentarily illuminates the two stretcher bearers in a freeze frame so that they appear to be a pair of unfortunates hauling a body across noman's land in the deadly glare of the flare. The paparazzi photographer continues firing off his camera flash, taking a few dozen money shots to flog to the newspapers when the body is named in the morning news. Considering he's the only snapper here, he's in for a few grand. The Garda who tipped him off will no doubt get a little taste of that payday as well.

By the time they get to the back of the ambulance, Joe's legs are on fire, and his lower back is going into a muscle spasm of protest at the treatment it's receiving. Hagan's body is accustomed to the routine and repetitive abuse of carrying corpses of all shapes and sizes up and down stairs, up and down hills, out of waterlogged ditches, out of burned buildings, out of mangled cars, out of the woods, across train tracks, across rivers, across canals, across vast windswept beaches in the night with the sea crashing all around and gulls circling above unseen in the fog and crying out in protest at their carrion being stolen away from them. But there is no tiredness in him. His body is surging with adrenaline as he carries his kill, his partial revenge for Molly. It fills him with joy, and he must do everything in his power to keep it from his face.

# CHAPTER SEVENTEEN

SPRING SUN GROWS stronger after its long winter absence. Joe likes the heat of it being magnified through the ambulance window onto his face. 'It's a lovely morning.'

'Lovely,' says Hagan in a tone that's so flat it's subterranean. He's not keen on hot weather when he's collecting bodies in place on open ground. The good weather facilitates insects and maggot infestation, especially in wooded areas, like the one he's heading to now, where carrion eaters such as crows, foxes and rats also become more active and can quickly devour the corpse, pulling it asunder and taking off with limbs that have to be tracked down and accounted for. He turns off the main road and eases along an old, disused country lane that became redundant many years ago when motorways were built through the area and bypassed the farmland that used to be here, follows what's left the old road into a strip of green belt that's been rezoned and bulldozed into being a brown belt building site for a new data storage centre. A large sign on the fenced-off entrance to the site brags about funding from the European Union's Development Fund. Avoiding potholes, he eases past giant yellow earth moving bulldozers and giant yellow trucks that dwarf the ambulance as it continues to make its way along to an acre-sized knot of old woodland that has survived development because there is a preservation order on it on account of it being the location of an ancient burial mound that dates back to the Battle of Clontarf in 1014.

He comes to a halt at a garda car parked up as an old uniformed sergeant gets out of it.

'Sergeant Flynn. How are you?'

'Still above the ground instead of below.' He looks to Joe. 'New lad?'

'Joe, this is Sergeant Flynn.'

Joe says quietly, 'Pleased to meet you.'

Flynn nods and looks to the woods. 'Fuckin fairy hill again,' and looks to Hagan, 'What do you make of all this?'

'I honestly have no idea,' Hagan says. 'Same as the others?'

'Exactly the same.'

'Do we have a name?'

'Not as yet.'

Hagan opens his morgue docket book, 'Who pronounced?'

'A young one. Jasis, what was her name now?'

'Doyle?'

'That was her,' says Flynn. 'Doctor Doyle. She looked sharp as a tack.'

'She is.'

'How's Frank holding up?'

'He's doing okay.'

'Do you go up to see him at all?'

'About once a fortnight.'

'Tell him I was asking after him and have him in my prayers.'

'I will.'

Flynn looks into the woods. 'You won't mind if I don't go in there with you. There's something about that mound that unsettles me.'

'No problem at all.' Hagan gets out of the ambulance, Joe does likewise, and they travel to the back of the ambulance to get a stretcher and a bodybag.

'Gloves,' Hagan says to Joe. Joe turns around and goes quickly back to the front of the ambulance to get a pair of gloves.

Flynn makes a smile. 'Is he any good?'

'His heart is in the right place.'

'But his head?' Flynn asks.

'Exactly.'

'I have the same problem with my rookie. Every time I look at him, he's got his nose in the fuckin phone. I left him on point at the body in there. Let him stew in it a little.'

Joe returns wearing a pair of gloves. Smiling.

130

'Let's go.' Hagan grabs the bodybag.

Joe grabs the stretcher and follows him into the woods.

The bodymen make their way along a narrow, muddy path winding its way through the circle of bramble bushes that stand like the first line of a maze defence protecting some ancient encampment. The earth dips and rises again, where a defensive moat was dug around the mound. As they go deeper into the heart of the wood, the main artery splinters into offshoots of ever smaller veins under the canopy that the sunlight finds it difficult to penetrate. It gets darker. It gets quieter. Here and there, amongst the silent trees, black circular burn patches adorned by rings of discarded cans, bottles, styrofoam takeaway boxes, plastic knives, forks, spoons, cups, bags, cardboard pizza boxes, crisp bags and sweet wrappers scar the ground.

Then, all at once, the grand mound of the fairy hill is in front of them. On top of it stands a giant ancient oak grown out from the pile of war dead buried there a millennium ago. Its trunk, battle-scarred by generations of kids who carved their names into its bark, stands fast, its limbs reaching out in all directions, forming a protective shield that covers the burial mound and its immediate surroundings. A circle of its adult offspring stand like centurions, and young saplings shoot up in a genetically encoded instruction to continue the line of their ancestors that once covered this land. On one of the lower branches, a length of green nylon clothesline rope dangles. Below it is the body of a teenage male with the other half of the rope around his neck. He's dressed in a new sky-blue tracksuit with a Dublin GAA t-shirt, has perfectly groomed hair and looks athletic – like he played a bit. The only anomaly on the scene is that he is wearing spotlessly clean white socks – but no shoes. Hagan begins to list the items of clothing into the possessions docket, adding the yellow studded earing in the left ear, a watch with a yellow metal band and a yellow metal ring on the middle finger of his right hand.

Joe stands staring at the corpse, gripped by the portrait of absurdity.

Hagan says, 'Bodybag.'

It snaps Joe out of his trance a frees him from the orbit of the question that hangs over the body of every suicide like a siren calling the curious sailer to come see: Why?

Hagan is certain that death is much stronger than life and ravenous. The fact that some of us, for whatever reason, are drawn off course to abandon our life journey and enter into its realm of death is of no surprise to him. It's hard to stay alive. He wouldn't be still in the world if it were not for the fact that he must find the men who are responsible for Molly's death and kill them. He looks again at the tidy, terrible scene and notices another anomaly: no flies are present, and the foxes, rats, crows, and other carrion eaters have not come to the corpse even though it has been on the open ground for some hours. But he's seen this and other strange anomalies before; in the chaos of the universe, things sometimes do or do not happen for reasons unknown to us, and he finds comfort in the fact that we don't know everything about our world, our universe or ourselves.

A rustling in the bushes produces a plump young Garda emerging from a gap, fixing his belt and looking ripe and embarrassed. 'Sorry. I really needed to go.'

Hagan says, 'We've all been there.'

The Garda nods and looks at Joe, who would also like to go behind the bushes.

The Garda says. 'Weird, isn't it?'

'What's that?' Hagan asks.

'That he has no shoes on him.'

Hagan nods. 'And his socks are spotless...'

The Garda's brain goes into overdrive on that one.

Hagan says, 'Look up.'

'What?'

'Look up.'

The Garda looks up and there in the branches dangles a pair of trainers.

'Jesus. What's that all about?'

'Keep on looking,' Hagan tells him.

The Garda, and now Joe too, look up into the branches of the great tree.

The Garda squints his eyes and says, 'I see another pair.'

'So do I,' says Joe.

The Garda counts them. 'There's four pairs up there.'

Hagan nods. 'That's about right.'

The Garda and Joe stare at Hagan, waiting for an explanation.

Hagan says, 'I've picked up three other youngfellas from this same spot. And it turns out that they all knew each other.'

The Garda says, 'A suicide pact.'

Hagan says, 'I didn't say that.'

The Garda nods his head and looks at Joe. 'I bet that's what it is, though. What do you think?'

Joe's about to speak, but Hagan says, 'He doesn't have an opinion on the matter.'

Joe shuts his mouth and swallows the opinion he's about to give.

The Garda nods. 'I get you.'

Hagan says to the Garda, 'And you shouldn't voice your opinion either. Everything you say can be used in court.'

The Garda doesn't like that; it sounds like he's being cautioned. He's the one who is supposed to be cautioning people when he arrests them. He's memorised the official cautionary phrase and everything, ready for the day he might get to use it. But he keeps his mouth shut about it.

Hagan kneels beside the corpse to apply the identity bracelet that has John Doe written on it; he senses the dead boy and his dead friends close by and feels that they can see him, see that he is a murderer. He fixes the grommet of the bracelet into place. Joe comes to join him at the body, opens out the bodybag onto the stretcher and goes to the ankles.

Hagan takes the wrists, 'You ready? On three. One – two.'

They lift the corpse into the bodybag, zip it up, and strap it to the stretcher.

The Garda looks around the woods. 'Do yous get a weird feeling here?'

Hagan gives Joe a look to keep his mouth shut.

The Garda says, holding his hand in the air like a mystic monk, 'You can feel it all around here.'

Hagan nods to Joe, and they lift the stretcher and begin to journey back to the ambulance.

'What do I do?' The Garda asks.

Hagan winks at Joe and says to the Garda, 'I think you have to wait here until Sergeant Flynn says otherwise.'

The Garda looks around him. 'Fuck…'

Joe fights off a smile. He's never been in on a gag before. He's usually the butt of it. He feels good. He watches as the Garda goes back into the bushes, opening his belt.

Back at the ambulance they find Sergeant Flynn having a cigarette. 'Yous better get a move on. There's a few of them down at the site entrance trying to get up here. Think it's his family. I'll give yous an escort out.'

Hagan nods, and they quickly put the stretcher into the ambulance.

Flynn looks at the woods. 'Where the fuck is he?'

Hagan says, 'Maybe you should give him a shout.'

As Hagan starts his engine, Flynn puts his siren on, and his rookie comes bolting out of the woods like a golden retriever and jumps into the garda car.

At the gate to the building site, Hagan sees the gathering of about a dozen people who are being held back by the site security. Flynn puts on his sirens and lights and Hagan does likewise as they pass through the crowd of teenagers.

Further along the old lane, they exit onto the busy main road and travel under lights and sirens back to the morgue. Joe delivers more hot news straight from the presses of his phone. 'They've identified the body we picked up from the beach as Jeffery Chase.'

Hagan nods and wonders how long it will take them to find Harry Murphy's body. Not much longer, he guesses, and he hopes he will have time to kill Marcus Strauss and DJ Dennis.

Joe continues with his news report. 'Apparently, he had a secret drug problem.'

Hagan nods. The PR Machine is working as expected. That will actually help him. It will make Strauss and DJ Dennis behave as usual, with no changes in their daily lives that might draw attention from the curious press, who will be wondering if Jeffery did his drugs all on his own or did he have coke-buddies.

Joe gives some news analysis, 'Just goes to show that you can never judge the book by the cover.'

'Indeed, you can't.' Hagan drives. Fingers crossed.

# CHAPTER EIGHTEEN

IT'S HALF PAST one in the morning when Hagan rides Molly's e-scooter to the grounds of Marcus Strauss's Victorian Villa. Apart from a high privet hedge to prevent peasants from peeping in from the road and a black-rodded wrought iron gate adorned with golden fleur-de-lis, there's no security to speak of. To the left of the large gate is a smaller pedestrian gate with a keypad on its post. Strauss had texted the key-code to his buddy Jeffery Chase, and Chase had sent the code to his dealer, Harry Murphy, so that Murphy could make deliveries of drugs to them, and Hagan got the number along with everything else from Murphy's phone.

With latex-gloved fingers, he punches the four-digit code into the keypad. The lock snaps open with magnetic precision, and he quietly enters. The sensor-activated floodlights are turned off due to the foxes that prowl through the grounds, set them off at night and disturb the sleep of the house owner. Hence, the CCTV cameras are made redundant by the lack of light. To the side of the house is a path that leads to a back door near the kitchen for the domestic staff to come by once a day to clean the house and cook for its owner. This door is operated by the same code that opens the gates. He again enters the digits into the keypad and hears the interior mechanism of the lock make a series of tiny sounds as the moving parts unlock the bolt from its housing in the door frame. Gently pushing the door, its well-oiled hinges remain silent as he enters the dark kitchen and is surprised by the fact that the entirety of the back wall of the house is gone ... the vast expanse of the bay is before him in an uninterrupted high cliff view. The moon illuminates everything through the back wall that is made entirely of glass. He watches the moon, how serine it is. His heart is not beating as hard as it did on the other two murders.

Strauss's voice travels from a ground-floor room at the front of the house. 'What the fuck are we going to do?'

'I have a few suggestions for a replacement,' another voice says.

'They have to be an agent.'

'Really? Why?'

Strauss says, 'The whole fucking point of the show is that Jack or Jill Nobody gets voted to stardom by thousands of other nobodies who pay premium rates on their phones to vote, and we make our money. If we don't have an agent to take the winner on the books, how the fuck do we sell the bullshit?'

'Of course, you're right. You know this shit. I'm just a fucking DJ.'

'Dennis, you're more than just a DJ, my friend.'

It's the kind of talk where one person speaks, and the other person waits for them to stop, like old-fashioned CB radio chatter – an internet conversation without the *10-4 Good Buddy*.

'Listen,' says DJ Dennis, 'Have you been able to get in touch with Harry?'

'No. I've tried him, but the junkie fuck is not picking up.'

'I'm nearly out of my supply here.'

'Maybe he's been arrested for being a drug dealing scumbag?'

'No,' says DJ Dennis. 'I'd know if he was nicked.'

'How?'

'I got to know that detective when we had that little problem. She listens to my show.'

'You need to be very careful there, my friend,' Strauss says. 'A cop is a cop.'

'She's cool. Believe me. Likes to do a few lines herself.'

'That makes me not trust her even more.'

'Anyway. She called me.'

'When?'

'This morning. She wanted to know if I'd heard from Harry.'

'And?'

'Well. No, I haven't. But the point is that she would know if he was locked up.'

'True. Why is she looking for him?'

'He's probably her fucking dealer.'

Strauss laughs, 'Fucking great. We're scoring our shit from a cop's rat.'

'Well, it's just as well that we are, isn't it?'

'How do you mean?'

'We'd be rightly fucked if he didn't reach out to her with the problem we had with that little redhead.'

'True … Real damn shame that was. She was some piece of ass.'

Hagan holds himself tight so he won't roar. The blood pounds on his eardrums and makes his head numb. All of him, every atom of his being, wants to run into that room and beat Strauss to death with his bare hands.

DJ Dennis says, 'She was. Have you spotted anything of interest in the latest batch of wannabes?'

'One or two that show some promise.'

'Fuck. I really need to score soon, or I'll be out. Do you know anyone else who deals?'

'Fuck no. Why don't you ask your driver? He must know a few more sources, right?'

'Fuck it. I'll ask him.'

'Okay,' says Strauss. 'I'm officially fucking fucked and ready for sleep. Who's making arrangements for our stupid fucking dead friend?'

'Fuck knows. I'm staying well out of it.'

'What's your PR guy saying to you?'

'Turn up to the funereal with a *who knew* kinda vibe.'

'Right. Fuck it. I'm off to bed. Fuck off.'

'You fuck off too.'

They both laugh. Then silence. Strauss patters flat-footed to the kitchen.

Hagan slides to the other side of the island counter.

Strauss goes to the fridge, and its light illuminates his pale white round belly sticking out of his bathrobe as he mulls over the food.

Hagan contains his murderous rage and reminds himself that beating Strauss's brains out on the floor is not in the plan. Strauss moves some items around the fridge, ferreting for something and then makes a disgruntled grunt like a half-satisfied pig, sticks the something he found into his gob, closes the door and shuffles his way out of the kitchen, chewing as he goes, breathing heavily as he heaves his obese corpus up the stairs.

Hagan stays put until he hears loud pissing into the middle of the toilet bowl and then carefully moves to the hallway. The interior has been gutted so that the building is an empty carcass. He waits at the first step of the glass stairway, listening to the familiar snapping sound of pills being popped out of their tinfoil beds, three of them, followed by the tap running water to fill a glass and then the swallow, followed by the footfalls of a fat man plodding to his bed for a drug-induced semi-comatose sleep.

While Hagan waits, he runs over the conversation he overheard, pulling from it broken pieces of information that might be useful to him, and gathers that they still haven't found Murphy's body. That's good. But the things they said about Molly come into his head and start a wildfire in his mind that could burn down the world. He must think of something else. He wonders if Val will come back to him. He misses her terribly but is glad she's in Spain with her sister and not here while he's doing what needs to be done. He wouldn't be able to hide it from her. She can read him like a book and she wouldn't approve.

A long, jagged snore comes from the bedroom above. After a few moments, the snoring finds its groove and settles into a long, steady, uninterrupted rhythm. He begins his journey up the stairs. The upside of the glass stairway is that there are no creaking floorboards to alert the sleeper. As he makes his progress, he listens to the tune of the nasopharynx. Should it stop, he will know that the sleeper is awake, but there's no worry of that happening; the snore song goes on in its rhythm, the benzodiazepine blocking any primal survival instinct to wake, carrying the sleeper away like booty to the land of Morpheus. Hagan finds the fucker out cold in the bed, dressed in red silk pyjamas like a fucking bloated cardinal. He wants to pulverise the great red slug, but his murder must be staged as an act of autoerotic asphyxiation. He knows from cases he's dealt with in the past that this manner of death will be seen as accidental, and friends and family are unlikely to ask for an inquest and will be more than happy for the details to be kept quiet so as to move quickly to the funeral. For this reason, the staging of the corpse must leave nothing to chance. Thankfully, the ornate brass-railed headboard is sturdy enough to take the giant red slug's dead weight.

Now having a good platform to work from, a solid bare canvas, so to speak, on which to create his masterpiece, he considers his obese pig's eighteen stone of unruly and unpredictable fat, but that characteristic will suit Hagan's needs. Mentally assembling the moving parts of his plan, he opens his backpack and removes a four-foot ribbon of red silk. The choice of ligature is important. Having seen hundreds of various ligatures used in suicides by hanging, one thing is for sure: ligatures have meaning to the deceased and are chosen with great care: a father's strap, a husband's fishing line, a favourite bathrobe cord, a guitar lead, a pair of hiking boot laces, a dog leash, a clothesline – the list goes on. The red silk scarf was chosen because he'd seen it used twice in cases similar to the one he was about to present to the state pathologist. A silk scarf is a fetish item, so this will help to rule out suicide and the manner of death to be ruled as accidental. The similarity to previous cases will help ease it through the system.

One end of the silk is tied to the sturdy brass ball-headed bedpost and pulled tight as he makes a noose of the other end, slips it around the giant red slug's fat neck, and then gives a gentle tug to set it in place. The creature stays fast in its drug-induced sleep. Hagan moves to the end of the bed, grabs the thing by its ankles and then pulls it off the bed so that it slides. A long snore is cut off as eighteen stones of fat interact with gravity and close the noose fast, crushing the trachea and oesophagus with a satisfying crunch and closing off the left and right common carotid arteries. Hagan pulls hard on its ankles. There isn't any fight in it. Its eyes open wide in perfect silence because the seal of the noose is so tight that no air can pass through the larynx. The creature blinks frantically. Whatever it is seeing is entering its mind as a nightmare. Its body jerks like a rodeo horse trying to buck death. But it can still see and hear.

'Look at me! Look at me, you fat horrible bastard!'

Its eyes widen and bulge and fill with bloodshot as they fix on Hagan.

'I am her father, and I'm sending you to fuckin hell!'

The solid brass bed frame stands fast and firm as a testimony to the Victorian craftsmen who made it. Then Hagan smells the gathering of the ancients all around him, all soaked in battle blood, reeking of death and forever hungry for more killing.

'Take the fucker! Take him!'

After thirty seconds of feeble struggle, the big red shitbag slumps, but this murder is nowhere near complete. The brain is still alive, and the heart is still going a mile a minute. There's no need now for Hagan to hold the ankles anymore. He allows uninterrupted gravity to take over the task completely. Somewhere in the next three minutes, death will occur. The threshold for clinical death is the cessation of the beating heart and brain activity. The first is measured by the absence of a carotid pulse, and the second by the absence of pupillary light reflex, whereby the pupils remain fixed and dilated. But even though the conscious being that inhabited the body is now absent, the body itself is far from dead. It spasms as every single limb, organ, and nerve gives a last desperate fight for life. But in the instant that all life leaves the body, the absence is definite, and it seems absurd that this corpse ever had life in it.

After maybe twenty minutes of sitting quietly with his thoughts in waves of satisfaction, he opens his backpack and removes a forensically pristine large orange rubber dildo. With latex-gloved hands, he covers the dildo in lubricant and then inserts it into the rectum of the corpse and leaves it in place. He then smears lubricant onto the hands of the corpse and leaves the tube of lubricant on the bedside locker.

After all his business is done, he makes one final check of the scene of death to ensure everything is correct. Satisfied with his work, he makes his exit.

'What are the odds?' Joe asks Hagan.

'Odds?'

'That we're back over in Dalkey.'

'Probably the same as being in Tallaght three times in a week.'

Joe nods and looks out the window at the liquid silver sea shimmering in the morning sun. 'I wonder what it is this time.'

'I wonder,' says Hagan, driving his ambulance up the Vico Road and knowing exactly what they are attending to.

Joe looks again at the address on the morgue docket. 'It's one of the big houses.'

'Yep.'

Hagan slows as they approach the beautiful wrought iron gates now wide open. A uniformed garda stands in the driveway and waves them into the grounds.

Joe says, 'Wow,' wide-eyed like a child at the Christmas panto watching the lights rise on the magnificent set. 'Doesn't look real.'

The Victorian villa stands splendidly yellow on the cliff's edge with a perfect eggshell blue sky, making a backdrop like the worst attempt at a landscape painting.

'It's real.' Hagan says and manoeuvres the ambulance into position. A strange feeling begins to percolate in him. After a moment, he realises that it's satisfaction. He's forgotten that feeling. He used to feel like this when he sat in the theatre waiting for the curtain to rise when Molly performed the role of Annie. And then, all during the performance, he would be blissfully floating in a lake of pride as he watched her singing and dancing. After Molly was killed and Val left him after the funeral, he woke up the next morning alone and noticed that he was dead inside. He was simply a walking corpse. He decided to end the charade of living, and after some thought about how best to commit his suicide, he settled on draining himself out into the bath so as not to make a mess and thus leave behind a reasonably easy corpse for Frank to collect. But the moment he put the knife to his arm, he felt Molly's presence. He told himself it was wishful thinking. But then he saw her. She seemed confused and asked him, 'What happened to me?'

'I don't know,' he told her.

She said, 'But isn't that your job to find the cause, mechanism and manner of my death?

'Yes...'

She walked out, and he put down the knife. His job. He would do his job for his daughter, and like a stopped clock, he began to tick again.

Almost as quickly as he identifies the satisfaction growing in him, he begins to subdue it as he circles the crunching gravel driveway designed for horse carriages to enter and disembark their passengers at the grand stairs and then continue through the gates. As he manoeuvres the rear of the ambulance up to the marble steps, he sees a uniformed garda superintendent standing in the doorway of the house. She doesn't like the morgue ambulance showing up two days in a row on her turf. People will think that Dalkey is turning into a gangland underworld.

Joe looks out of the window. 'It must be terrible to die if you own all of this.'

Hagan inches into position. 'How do you mean?'

'Well, think about it,' says Joe. 'You're leaving so much behind you.'

Hagan scans the grounds for Gallagher. 'You know the drill. Right?'

'Got it.' Joe nods his head confidently. He's getting the hang of it now.

The pair of bodymen begin the well-oiled routine of getting the gurney and bodybag from the back of the ambulance. Joe takes care of the equipment, and Hagan deals with the superintendent. 'Good morning.'

She looks up to the sky to see if it is a good morning and then nods to him.

'What have we got?' he asks her.

She eyes the flowerbeds and the privet hedge as her well-honed garda senses suspect that nosey neighbours with big ears and bad intentions are lurking unseen. 'Come inside,' she says.

Hagan follows her with Joe hot on his heels.

In the daylight, Hagan can see that things were done, and nothing was spared in gutting the building and turning it into an open-plan Californian beach house. All of the interior walls were knocked out, and a Malibu view was added by knocking out the back walls and replacing them with glass so that the owner had a clear, uninterrupted view of the sea.

Joe's head spins back to the old Victorian door he came through as his mind grapples with the abrupt and incompatible architectural void between the two sensibilities that sit three hundred years apart. 'Wow. I wasn't expecting this in here.'

'Something else, isn't it?' says the superintendent, suddenly filled with pride for some unknown reason. 'Lovely and modrin and bright.'

'It's like an airport lounge or something,' Joe sighs.

She's not sure if that is a compliment. 'It's what they call the open plan.'

'Yeah?'

Hagan interrupts, 'Do we have a name for the deceased?'

'Oh, yes,' says the superintendent. 'It's Marcus Strauss.'

Joe takes a step back. 'No way. From the telly?'

'The same,' says the superintendent.

'But we just picked up Jeffery Chase.'

'Don't I know? Wasn't I there, sure? What are the odds?'

'That's what I said this morning,' Joe says and looks at Hagan. 'Didn't I say that?'

Hagan gives him a look.

She adds with a serious tone, 'And DJ Dennis came straight over when he heard. Very concerned, so he is. Over there in the kitchen, he is now. Upset, so he is. Terrible.'

Joe says in a loud whisper, 'DJ Dennis.'

The kitchen isn't a separate room. It's a smaller space divided from the larger space by an imaginary wall somewhere near the marble countertop. DJ Dennis and his chauffeur, Pike, sit on the other side of this imaginary wall, chatting and sipping coffee like they are performing a play about two innocent men on stage.

Joe pretends not to look at the biggest star in Ireland.

DJ Dennis turns his head to profile, somehow aware that he has an audience. For him, there is always the presence of the invisible fourth wall that the audience sits behind and watches him through, and he has trained himself to be aware of their presence. But if he were all that gifted at reading the room, he would know that a man is looking at him who intends to kill him.

Hagan feels his face turning red as his blood begins to boil. He cannot take his eyes off DJ Dennis, yet he knows he mustn't look at him.

'Wow,' says Joe to the superintendent. 'Did you see the show last week when he waved the magic wand to send through that girl to the final.'

'I did. I did,' says the superintendent, 'But to be honest, I didn't think that the girl was all that good meself.'

Joe nods. 'Maybe he just saw something in her that he liked. You know, he's very good at working with the emerging talent, they say.'

'They say that, true enough. They say that alright, so they do.'

'Is the fella with him famous too?' Joe asks.

'No, no.' says the superintendent, 'That's his chauffeur. I think he's kind of like his bodyguard as well, if you get me.'

Joe nods. 'Have you spoken with DJ Dennis?'

'Oh, we had a bit of a chat when I arrived on the scene. It was himself who discovered the body. Poor man.'

Joe nods. 'Probably wasn't a good time to ask him for a selfie.'

'What do you mean?'

'The two of you, you know, like a picture with you both in it so you can prove to people that you met him.'

'Right. Right. Is that thing now?'

'Yeah. Everyone does it if they meet a famous person, and then you post it on your insta or whatever and get likes.'

'I didn't know that. It's all goin on all around us, isn't it?'

'A fella got thirty thousand likes in one day because he got a selfie with Lilly-Bitty the night before she died.'

She thinks, 'Didn't she win last season of A Star is Born?'

'She did,' says Joe.

She thinks. 'And that would have been the last known picture of Lilly-Bitty alive then.'

'Exactly.'

'Well, that would make it a very special picture, right enough,' she says.

'Imagine if you got a selfie with DJ Dennis, and then he died.'

Hagan says, 'We have all the information that we need. Can someone show us to the body?'

'Right,' says the superintendent, 'I better do it myself. If you want it done right, and all of that. Isn't that what they say?' She turns to the almost invisible glass staircase.

Hagan asks, 'Upstairs?' Because he should have no idea where the body is.

'Yes,' says the superintendent, leading them up the grand glass spiral.

'We're going to have to be very careful coming back down,' Hagan tells Joe. 'Glass steps are lethal.'

Joe follows Hagan and looks back to see that DJ Dennis's eyes are fixed on him. He feels a sudden rush of blood that makes him a little dizzy and fearful, and he quickens his pace to keep up with Hagan.

Inside the bedroom, the body of Marcus Strauss is lying on the silk sheeted bed, attired in fresh blue silk pyjamas with his hands tidy across his chest, laid out like a bishop. It would look like the scene of a quiet and peaceful passing of a pure soul if it weren't for the loud purple ligature marks that are glaring around the neck of the corpse.

Hagan cannot believe that someone has come in and fucked up his presentation. He wants to roar but stays calm and asks the superintendent, 'I can't but notice the ligature marks around the neck.'

She nods, 'Yes. Is that what they are? I wasn't sure myself and said that would be a thing for the pathologist to look at. I didn't want to jump to any conclusions.'

Hagan nods. 'Someone's arranged the body?'

The superintendent shakes her head, 'Arranged? Good God, no.' She knows enough about the law to know that arranging dead bodies on their scenes of death is against the law. She says, 'DJ Dennis found him. The poor man was so distraught that he called his chauffeur to come up and make him presentable.'

Hagan can smell the cover-up shit that he's stepped into. He backs his way out of it, 'I meant laid him out.'

She smiles, 'Laid him out. Yes. I'd imagine so. They wanted to give him a bit of dignity.'

Hagan asks, 'So they called the ambulance after they dignified him?'

She examines that for a moment. She can smell the attitude in it. 'We're not entirely sure of the sequence of events and the timeline. I've yet to go through it with DJ Dennis himself. He's very upset. He might even have to cancel his radio show today.'

Hagan starts to bury his attitude as deep as it can go. 'So, just for the records. Who called the ambulance?'

'I think DJ Dennis called a friend of his in the force, and she put the wheels in motion.'

Hagan knows the friend in the force is Gallagher. He gets right off the subject because he's finding it hard to bury his rage. He nods and readies his morgue docketbook. 'Who pronounced death?'

The superintendent shifts a little, 'Well. We're keeping a low profile on it.'

Hagan begins to realise the nature of the fuckup attempt at a cover-up. 'There was no doctor called?'

'We called an ambulance. Sure, the rigor mortis was set into him when we got here.'

'So death has not been pronounced?'

'The paramedic said he was dead.'

'A paramedic is not qualified to pronounce death.' He closes his docketbook.

The superintendent is becoming annoyed with her authority being questioned. 'Give him a good shake then and see if he wakes up. Jesus, all this fussing and fiddling with dockets. Just do your job, man. Take the body out of here.'

Hagan says, 'I need to make a call.' And walks out of the house. Joe quickly follows him.

Outside, away from the ears, Hagan calls the morgue and Kunis answers. He says, 'I need to speak with her.'

Kunis says, 'She's in the middle of a post-mortem.'

'Just put the phone on speaker.'

He waits and listens as Kunis walks to the State Pathologist Doctor Cullen, who is performing an autopsy, and tells her, 'It's Hagan, Ma'am.'

'What is it, William?' Cullen asks him.

'This Dalkey body is not pronounced.'

There's a moment of silence. Then Cullen says, 'Leave the scene.'

'Got it.' Hagan hangs up and nods to Joe. 'We're out of here. Keep your mouth shut.'

As Hagan starts the engine he sees the superintendent's angry face appear at his window.

She says, 'Where do you think you're going?'

'The body is not pronounced dead.'

'Don't you dare drive away from here. I'm ordering you to take that body from the house.'

'I take my orders from a higher authority than the police.'

'Nobody is above the law.'

'That's very true.' He feels himself getting annoyed. 'And that applies to the gardai as much as to anybody else. The law states that the body must be pronounced dead by a doctor certified by the Irish Medical Board and appointed to the duty by the coroner's office. And it is the coroner who holds the highest warrant in the State. So, one of us is standing very much outside of the law. Now, if you'll excuse me, I have other dead waiting to be collected.'

Hagan eases the ambulance back out through the gate and gets sight in his mirrors of DJ Dennis standing at the front door of the house and holding his hands in the air in protest. Hagan wants to stop the ambulance, get out, and beat DJ Dennis to death. He keeps on driving away. At the same time, the superintendent's phone rings, and as she listens to the call, her face begins to turn pale.

Hagan drives out of the gates and back out of Dalkey along the beautiful coast roast.

'What happens now?' Joe asks.

Hagan says, 'We have a job waiting. We'll do it, and if everything that needs to be done back there is done right, we will go back and remove the body.'

Joe can sense that Hagan is annoyed, but he dares not ask him about it. He looks out the window.

Hagan knows he needs to lighten his mood. He's murderous, and his anger is seeping out of him like odorous sweat. He says, 'Are you hungry?'

'Starvin.'

'There's a garage on the way that does the best sausage rolls.'

Ten minutes later, as they eat their jumbo sausage rolls and drink their tea in the petrol station forecourt, Hagan asks Joe, 'What kind of music do you like?'

'Indie.'

Hagan has no idea what that means. 'You got it on your phone?'

'Yeah.'

'Put something on there.'

Joe searches through his phone. 'I think you'll like this one.'

A frantic guitar kicks in like a kid skateboarding down a hill the wrong way in traffic and is hit with a chaotic burst of drums. It sounds like pumped-up punk on speed, but then the rhythm settles into a 12-bar blues and a long riff. A guy howls about love and death. It becomes music.

Joe examines Hagan's face for clues. 'What d'you think?'

'I like it.'

Joe smiles. Nods.

They play music until they arrive at the next pick-up at an old folks' home, content with sausage rolls and hot tea in their bellies and the memory of music in their ears. Hagan's empathetic disposition returns and Joe feels he is back on his adventure.

As they enter the lobby with the gurney, Joe says, 'This is like the place me Nana was in.'

'Yeah? Was she in it long?'

'No. A few weeks only. But they still got half of the value of her house.'

'How was that?'

'The fair deal scheme. Me ma had to sign me Nana's house over to the home, so when she died, it was sold, and they took half of the money.'

'Doesn't sound like much of a fair deal if she was only in the place for a few weeks.'

'We had to live in a hotel for a few weeks until we found a place to rent.'

'Rough time for you then.'

Joe nods.

Hagan nods, too. He's done enough work in these homes to know that some of the old stock take to it and settle in for the long haul, and others don't. There's probably no scientific reason why one person should thrive while another fails under the same conditions.

They're met by the beaming smile of a small, middle-aged nurse with a kind round face, dressed in a salmon-pink uniform and pink trainers. 'Good morning. How are you today? I'm Nurse Imelda. Welcome.'

'Morning, Nurse Imelda. I'm William, and this is Joe.'

She gives Joe a double take and then touches him on the arm. 'How are you, Joe?'

Joe looks at Hagan and then looks back to Nurse Imelda. 'Fine. Thanks.'

She rubs his arm. 'Okay. Okay. That is good. This way, please.' She walks into the interior.

Joe pushes the gurney along with no idea that he is still wearing the death of his nana on his sleeve. Hagan spotted it during his first day in the morgue. It's probably what has endeared him to him.

The pair of blue-suited bodymen follow the pink-scrubbed nurse along the pastel-coloured corridor, past the active elderly area, the day room, the art classes, the keep fit by waving your arms in the air from the safety of your chair classes to Abba. They follow the fast moving white shoed feet through a set of doors and along the corridor for those who are high maintenance, shouting, fighting it, disorderly. Then, through a set of secure doors and onto the floor for those who are no bother to anyone. As they pass these rooms, old, expressionless, simple, childlike faces look out at them like blank sheets of paper.

Joe says, 'You think they'd close the doors.'

Hagan says, 'If you have to be in a room on this ward, it's better for the door to be open.'

Nurse Imelda stops at the door with the triskele pinned on it. 'In here,' she says quietly and opens the door. They enter to find the corpse of an old lady in her bed dressed up to the nines in a splendid black evening dress and make-up and jewels, looking like she's ready to get up from her deathbed and take off to the opera.

Hagan asks, 'You've prepared her?'

'No,' Nurse Imelda says, 'She dressed herself like that in the middle of the night.' She gestures to the wardrobe that is full of posh gowns. 'She loved her dresses. Made them all herself. She was a seamstress most of her working life.'

That makes sense to Hagan. The woman's death may have come unexpectedly to the medical staff, but it did not come unexpectedly to her. She has met it with elegance. She is very much still in the room. 'The dress is beautiful,' he says so she can hear it.

'It is,' Nurse Imelda agrees.

Hagan begins his paperwork routine with the morgue docket. 'Name?'

Nurse Imelda says, 'Elizabeth Duggan. Very nice lady. A long time resident.'

Hagan nods. He knows that translates into Nurse Imelda having known Elizabeth for a long time and is, in her own way, grieving. There's no room for that information on his docket. 'We'll take good care of her.'

Nurse Imelda nods and says, 'The rosary beads are going with her, and the Saint Christopher medal pinned to her gown is going with her also.'

Hagan writes it into the possessions docket and says, 'I see pearl earrings?'

'They are also going with her,' Nurse Imelda says, 'And her make-up bag. She was very particular about her lips and eyes, as you can see, and she requested that the undertaker use her own make-up on her. She wants to be buried in this dress.'

'A woman who knew what she wanted.' He takes out his notebook and writes into it. 'I'll make a note of that and make sure that undertaker gets it.'

'Thank you.'

'Rings?' Hagan asks.

'Her family have them. She wants them passed on.'

'Good,' Hagan says.

These items must be accounted for because their emotional importance to the family cannot be measured. The loss of an old lady's wedding and engagement rings cannot be replaced with a voucher for the local jeweller.

Nurse Imelda says, 'The family also want to know if you can keep her woolly socks on.'

Hagan looks to the bright pink fluffy socks poking out from beneath the elegant gown. 'Of course,' he says, writing that the socks stay on her in his notebook. He asks Nurse Imelda, 'Can we take the sheet?'

Imelda lowers her voice, 'Yes…'

The administrators of the homes don't like them taking the sheet that the deceased is lying on. It's an unnecessary cost.

Nurse Imelda asks, 'Can I bring her husband in before you take her.'

'Of course…' Hagan is surprised that the goodbyes have not been completed, but he doesn't pass any comment.

Nurse Imelda tells him, 'He's also a resident. He doesn't remember anymore, but you know, we don't really know – do we?'

'No, we don't,' Hagan says.

Nurse Imelda exits with a swish, leaving a scent of freshly washed linen and sweet wildflowers in her wake.

Joe has not taken his eyes off the corpse in the bed. He says, as if suddenly out of breath, 'I might pop to the toilet and–'

'Stay,' Hagan tells him. 'Sit down if you have to, but don't walk out on her.'

'I don't think I can…'

'Sit down there,' Hagan tells him.

Joe sits in the chair beside the bed and looks at the floor.

'You'll be fine,' Hagan tells him.

Joe doesn't look up.

The door opens, and Nurse Imelda wheels in a frail old man dressed in pyjamas. His wide blue eyes look at everything in wonder as she wheels him to the bedside.

No one speaks. Mister George Duggan stares at his wife in the bed; his expression doesn't change, and then his eyes travel to a black and white picture beside the bed. The moment was captured outside the GPO in O'Connell Street and it shows a young couple in the prime of their life, stopping on their way to watch a movie in one of the great cinemas that once lit up the city. It's hard to tell if the couple in the picture are fifteen or twenty-five. By today's standards, they look like children wearing adult clothing because it was a moment in time before the existence of teenagers. These were the people who were born during WW2, a time when working-class children in Dublin worked and earned a living. Mister Duggan smiles and takes the picture and examines it closely. What he's looking at is a badge on the lapel of his jacket, a badge awarded to apprentices who worked for the State's public transport company, CIE. And it's a badge that makes him a good catch to the girl on his arm, a badge he recognises. 'Coras Iompair Eireann,' he says.

Nurse Imelda doesn't know what he means.

Hagan nods to him. 'You worked on the trains then?'

Mister Duggan makes a brush-holding gesture with his hand like Caravaggio. 'I painted the livery on the coaches.'

Nurse Imelda smiles. 'I never knew that.'

Hagan nods. 'That was beautiful work.'

Hagan feels Elizabeth Duggan standing beside him, looking at her husband, radiating pure love distilled over a lifetime and free from the pollutants of the trivia, petty arguments, and disagreements about once-important matters that are now long forgotten. Everything is forgotten and cleansed, and all that is left is immaculate love. For a moment, Hagan thinks of Val and his love for her and the love she has for him, and he wonders if they will ever be able to stand in the same room at the same time ever again. He pushes the painful thought away and almost feels the reassuring hand of death on his shoulder, promising that it will eventually come for him and take away all the pain.

Mister Duggan delves back into the picture and a timeless Saturday night where he is forever out on a date with his love, smelling of Brylcreem that slicks his hair and Old Spice aftershave, wearing his big brother's hand-me-down suit and winkle picker shoes, and feeling like a prince of Dublin with his princess on his arm.

They wait.

After a few moments, Hagan and Nurse Imelda exchange a look. She says, 'Thank you.'

She turns the wheelchair and wheels Mister Duggan out with the picture in his hands.

Hagan looks at Joe, who is sitting in a heap in the chair, in rag order, holding his face in his hands and making little snotty sobs that drip down onto the tiled floor.

Hagan says, 'Right. Let's take care of her.'

Hagan fixes the name bracelet to the wrist birdlike wrist. Then, he carefully untucks the bottom bedsheet and wraps it around the body to form a shroud. He tells Joe, 'Open the bodybag and spread it out on the gurney.'

Joe sniffles and gets on with it. Doing something useful is making him feel better. When the bodybag is fully opened, Hagan says, 'You take the feet.'

Taking either end of the shrouded corpse, they lift it so that it is hammocked in the bedsheet and carefully bring it to the bodybag, where they gently lower it into place. All that done, Hagan zips it up. The elasticated edges of the black stretcher cover are then fitted around the gurney so that the bodybag and its contents are completely and respectfully covered from view.

Hagan points to a box of hankies beside the bed and says to Joe. 'Blow your nose and wipe your face.'

Joe blows his nose like the fog horn on the sinking Titanic.

Hagan waits while his rookie sorts himself out. 'You ready?'

Joe nods.

They wheel the body out and through the corridors. Curious heads look up from beds and strain in their chairs. No one in here is a stranger to death. When they get to the main lobby, a guard of honour, comprised of staff and residents with mobility, has formed in the lobby. At the doors stands Nurse Imelda next to Mister Duggan in his wheelchair, still clutching the framed Saturday night date. As Hagan and Joe pass close with the remains, a few staff members bless themselves, and a few residents wave goodbye.

With the remains of Elizabeth Duggan in the ambulance, Hagan drives at a respectful, slow speed out of the grounds of the home. Once on the road, he returns a missed call from dispatch and is told that the remains of Marcus Strauss are now clear to be removed.

On the drive back to Dalkey, Joe asks, 'We collect sudden and unexpected deaths to see if they are murders, right?'

'We do.'

'So why are we taking the body of Elizabeth Duggan?'

'Well, just because she was old doesn't mean she was expected to die, does it?'

Joe thinks about that, 'I guess. But she probably just died of old age.'

'And it's the *probably* bit that's the problem. Manner of death being *probably* natural doesn't cut it.'

'But she wasn't murdered. Right?'

'How do you know? There's plenty of people out there who murder old relatives to get the inheritance.'

Joe nods.

Hagan says, 'And it's not only murder that the coroner is looking for. There's four manners of death, you have to remember.'

'Right'

'Go on,' says Hagan. 'Name them.'

Joe says without having to think, 'Natural, accidental, suicide and homicide.'

'Right. What about accidental? She could have fallen. But in the case of a care home, that's a liability issue. So maybe someone pops her back in the bed and makes it all look good?'

Joe's eyes widen. 'I get it.'

'Or maybe someone mixed up the medication? Accidental overdose?'

Joe nods. It's all falling into place for him. 'I'd say that happens a lot.'

'And these poor old souls can't stand up for themselves, can they?'

'No.'

'So that's why we have the remains of Elizabeth Duggan in the ambulance. We're looking after her.'

Joe feels a smile grow on his face and starts to feel better about it all. He likes looking after people who can't look after themselves.

Back in Dalkey, the Sun is giving its best effort, but it's a meagre offering compared to what it gives out to the continental mainland of Europe and the rest of the world. However, it's the normal ration of sunshine for Europe's little island outpost. Hagan once more drives through the gates of Strauss's mansion and immediately notices that there has been a serious and dramatic change in personnel. A white Garda Technical Bureau van is parked beside an unmarked detective car in the driveway.

Hagan says to Joe, 'Don't have anything to say to anyone. Someone asks you a question, you refer them to me. Yeah?'

'Okay.'

'I mean it. Don't be fucking making conversation with anyone like you were this morning. We don't do that. Do you understand me?'

'Yes. Is there something wrong?'

'It just got serious. We've already been here. Keep your mouth shut. Tight.'

'Got it.'

As Hagan parks up, he feels the blood in his head turn to hot oil when he sees Detective Gallagher making her way over to him. Sweat forms on his forehead, and he knows he better cool it. He smiles. 'Surprised to see you here.'

'Don't even go there,' she says to him. 'How do I get these calls? Someone has rattled the Minister's cage. What happened the last time you were here?'

Hagan sees DJ Dennis out of the corner of his eye, standing at the front door and makes sure that he doesn't look at him because he is sure that Gallagher would read his murderous intentions.'Deceased wasn't pronounced.'

'And what did your one, the Superintendent, say to you?'

Hagan knows that Gallagher is trying to determine if the Superintendent mentioned Gallagher's name or DJ Dennis having contacted a friend on the force. 'Not much apart from a friend of the deceased had made an effort to give him some dignity.'

'And that's it?' Gallagher searches his face for any clues that he is holding back on.

'That's it.' Hagan gives her his best poker face, making a huge effort to keep his anger towards her in a place where she can't see it.

She nods. 'Techies are up the walls in there. Saying someone arranged the body and removed artefacts. You know about that?'

Hagan pretends to think. 'I noted the ligature marks on the neck alright. But the Superintendent was present, so I assumed she had it all in hand.'

'Don't even talk to me about that stupid inbred fuckin egit. She's after making a right dog's fuckin dinner of it there. When the State Pathologist called her, she told her it was *her* crime scene. Did Doctor Cullen say anything to you about that?'

'I wouldn't be in that circle. It's a couple of floors above my pay grade.'

'Of course. You're like meself. A fucking grunt. Anyway, body's all cleared and ready for you.'

Hagan watches her walk away from him straight to DJ Dennis. As he watches them talking, he feels that someone is watching him and looks around to see DJ Dennis's chauffeur, Pike, standing by his limo and staring at him. For a moment, they make eye contact. Hagan breaks off and hopes he hasn't shown his hand.

Up in the master bedroom, Gallagher is standing at the glass wall looking out into the bay.'This is the life, huh?'

Hagan nods.

She makes a crooked smile, 'Looks like a fuckin office block, if I'm to be honest. But what would I know?'

Hagan nods and takes in the corpse that is still in place on the bed, but a brown paper evidence bag is now in place beside it.

Gallagher follows his eye-line and says, 'Right. The evidence bag. Apparently, after an interview with the person who discovered the body, and that's a whole other can of fuckin worms that I do not want to get into, it transpired that, along with the ligature, another item of interest was removed from the scene. She reads the evidence bag, 'Item A - sex toy.' She says to Joe, 'That's posh talk for a big dildo.' She smiles and reads him. His face is glowing red. She says to him, 'You know what that's all about, don't you?'

Joe looks at Hagan.

Hagan says to him, 'Don't mind her.'

She nods and smiles. 'He's the sensitive type. I get it. Anyway, It was up his arse…' She looks at Joe again.

Joe looks away.

She says to Joe, 'You're a dark horse. I can tell.' She says to Hagan, 'So we're looking at auto-erotic asphyxiation gone wrong. And since this item was on the body, well, *in the body,* to be correct, it travels with it to the morgue. That will be an interesting entry into your personal possessions docketbook.'

Hagan begins to fill it in. 'I've had stranger ones.'

'Really?'

Hagan nods.

'What's the fuckin strangest one?'

Hagan thinks.

She reads him … 'On second thoughts, I don't want to know.'

He nods.

'It would have given me nightmares, wouldn't it?'

He nods. 'Doctor who pronounced?'

'Barry Dunne.'

'Have the deceased been officially identified?'

'Yeah. His assistant made identification.'

Hagan nods. 'You're the on scene?'

'Fuck no. Eh…' She thinks. Then shouts down the stairs, 'Who can hear me?'

No one answers.

She shouts again, 'Is it a room full of fucking deaf fuckers down there?'

A young male voice carefully answers, 'I can hear you, Sergeant?'

She looks at Hagan, 'What is it about rookies that makes you want to hold them under the water until they stop making bubbles?' She looks at Joe. Then she shouts back down the stairs, 'What's your name?'

'Sean Mooney, Sergeant.'

'Okay, Mooney. You're the on scene for this one.'

'I'm still on probation, Sergeant.'

'No one gives a fuck.' She looks back to Hagan. 'Put down Sean Mooney.'

Hagan scribbles the name into the docket.

Then she slides out the wildcard tormenting her investigative mind, 'What are the odds?'

Joe is about to explain how he said that this morning, but he remembers what Hagan told him and keeps his mouth shut—tight.

Hagan keeps on writing like he doesn't know what she means. 'Odds?'

Detectives, especially homicide detectives, don't like coincidences. In fact, as a rule, they don't believe in them. They don't allow the possibility of coincidence into their investigative theory. When they hear a suspect use the word coincidence, it is like waving a red flag at a bull.

She says, 'Jeffery Chase and now Marcus Strauss – both work on the same TV show.'

Hagan knows that the two dead men have much more in common, and he knows that she knows it. But what she is trying to do here is figure out if Hagan knows their connection to Molly's death. She throws out the baited hook. 'Some fuckin coincidence, huh?'

Hagan feels a surge in him that's not entirely under his control. He looks her straight and tells her, 'There's no such thing as coincidence.'

She keeps looking back at him. 'That's what I think too.' She steps a little closer to him to get his scent. 'What do you call it then?'

Hagan is now freely oozing his murderous sweat, and he doesn't give a fuck if she smells it off of him. 'The only thing that I know for sure is that for every action in the universe, there is an opposite and equal reaction…'

She reads him. 'That's an interesting theory.'

'It's not a theory,' he says.

'No? What is it?'

'It's a law.'

'Really? I thought I knew all the laws.'

'Newton's third law of motion,' he says and then remembers to smile.

She reads him and smiles back. 'Good one.' But she's gone cold on the banter. 'I'll let you get on with it.' She walks back down the stairs. Her mind works flat out. Did he just tell her that he knows all of the circumstances surrounding his daughter's death? Did he just tell her that he's killing the men involved? For the first time in her career, she's light-headed with adrenalin.

Hagan watches her go and then looks at Joe, who looks lost. 'Don't mind any of that. Just a bit of banter,' he says.

Joe nods.

'Let's get on with it.' Hagan doesn't care now if she suspects him because she won't be able to stop him before he gets to DJ Dennis, who he's going to kill in the morning. He fixes the name tag on the wrist of the corpse and thinks. 'It's heavy. So we need to be mindful of our backs here.' Moving the bedside locker away from the bed, he creates a clear space on the floor. 'Fold up that sheet out of the way.'

Joe sets about it.

Hagan spreads the bodybag out on the floor alongside the bed. 'We'll use the bottom sheet just like we did with Elizabeth. Yeah?'

Joe nods and watches Hagan wrap the fat wax grey corpse in the silk sheet. Then, taking each end of the hammock, they ease it off the bed and into the bodybag. Despite their best efforts, it lands with a solid thud. The two evidence bags containing the ligature and the sex toy are added into the bag, and it's zipped up. They then strap and stretcher the remains and bear them down the stairs. Carefully.

The body of Marcus Strauss is put into the ambulance next to the remains of Elizabeth Duggan.

Hagan starts the ambulance, lights it up, and gets out of there.

# CHAPTER NINETEEN

HAGAN RETURNS TO the leafy haven of Ferndale nestled into the foot of the Dublin Mountains.

Joe is glued to the window. 'I've never seen the mountains up this close.'

Although Hagan has a hundred other things on his mind about the crime scene he created and is now about to attend, he cannot believe what Joe is saying. 'Are you telling me that you've never been up to the Sally Gap or the Hell Fire Club?'

'What's the Hell Fire Club?'

'Holy Jesus. How can you live your whole life in Dublin and not have been up the mountains?'

Joe shrugs. 'Don't have a car.'

'They have buses.'

Joe shrugs. 'I don't like buses. I get travel sick on them. What's the Hell Fire Club?'

'What about days out with the school?'

'I wasn't allowed to go on them.'

'Why not?'

'I got bullied.'

'Bullied? You're fucking huge.'

'That's why I got bullied. But I didn't want to go on the bus as well. What's the Hell Fire Club?'

Hagan shakes his head. 'I'll explain later. Okay, we're just up here past this bend.'

As they round the bend in the narrow road, they come to the gate with a garda car parked outside. A cluster of hungry news crews turn the cameras on to the morgue ambulance.

Joe unconsciously fixes his hair. 'Why is the news here?'

'Must be someone important in there.'

'How do they know what it is when we don't?'

'They have better contacts than we do.'

Joe reads that answer. 'Will we be on the news?'

'Probably.'

Joe begins to smile.

'Please don't fucking smile.'

'Sorry.' Joe puts on a straight face and beams at the cameras with wide eyes.

'Just look at the floor. Pretend you're doing paperwork,' Hagan tells him.

'Right.' Joe looks at the floor, grabs a pen from his pocket and twirls it in his fingers.

'What are you doing?'

'Pretending.'

'Pretending what?'

'That I'm doing paperwork. I need a pen, or else they will think I'm just looking at the floor for no reason.'

'God fucking help me.' Hagan stops at the garda car that's blocking the gate and waits.

Joe improves his performance by making a face like he's concentrating on something important and then nodding to himself.

The garda in his car looks up from his phone and is surprised to see the morgue ambulance looming in his window. He quickly starts his engine and puts the car into gear. It lurches forward and conks out. Sniggers ripple through the press pack. The garda has another go, and then, taking more care, he eases the car along until the entrance into the property is clear. The ambulance enters. Joe continues his acting debut.

Hagan sees two technical bureau vans and two detective cars parked inside the grounds as he reverses his ambulance to the front door.

'Strange,' says Joe.

160

'What's that?' asks Hagan as he checks his mirror and gauges his distance, but he also sees Gallagher sitting in her unmarked car and texting on her phone.

Joe says, 'The upstairs window is all blacked out with something.'

'Flies,' Hagan says and gets out of the ambulance.

What Joe's just heard makes no sense to him. 'Flies?' He gets out of the ambulance and makes his way to the back of it, looking all the time at the upstairs window, and now he sees that the blackness that covers it is moving on the inside of the windowpanes and realises that the window is indeed curtained with flies...

At the back of the ambulance, Hagan has the doors open and is already pulling out the kit that they will need for this one. 'Do you hear that?'

Joe looks at the house and listens to a distinctive buzz-hum from the dark interior. 'What is it?'

'Carrion flies,' Hagan says, 'Millions of them.'

'Carrion?'

'Flesh eaters,' Hagan says.

'I didn't know about flesh-eating flies.'

'Every day is a school day. Right?'

'But I hate flies.'

'Yeah?'

'Yeah. I really hate them.'

'Well, if you ever meet a person who likes them, run away.'

'We're not going in there. Are we?'

'Well – that's where the body is.'

'Right. Will they not get the flesh eaters out first?'

'Who would do that job?'

'The garda.'

'How would they do it?'

'Open the doors. Whoosh them out.'

'Whoosh them?'

'Yeah.'

'Those flies will fight to the death to stay on that body. Don't worry – we're getting fully suited up.'

'What if I have a phobia about flies?'

'A fly phobia?'

'Yeah.'

'Do you have a fly phobia?'

'I don't know. I might.'

'You don't.'

'How would I know? I've never been in a house full of flesh eaters before.'

'I'm telling you that you don't have a fly phobia.'

'Right. How do you know?'

'I'm trained to spot these kinds of things.'

'Right. What are the signs then of a fly phobia?'

'A fella who has a fly phobia would have run out of the gate by now.'

Joe looks at the gate. Too late for that now, he thinks. 'Right.'

Hagan takes out two heavy-duty white suits, adds goggles, a mask, booties, heavy-duty elbow-length blue rubber gloves and white wellingtons to the ensemble and tells Joe, 'Suit up.'

Joe climbs into his plastic battledress, trying to imagine what is to come, and envisions near future humanity fighting for survival in the apocalyptic war of the flesh-eating flies and the entire planet covered in a suffocating carpet of hungry wriggling flesh-eating larvae. He tries to stop thinking about it because it's making him panic. He's wishing now that he didn't eat that second breakfast that his mother always cooks in the morning, saying to him that the second breakfast is for her but then saying that she's not in the humour for it and he should eat it or it will go in the bin, and it is a sin to waste food. He always eats the second breakfast. There would be no second breakfasts in the dystopian flesh fly apocalypse. Hagan's voice halts his runaway train of THE FLESH EATERS!

'Earth calling Joe. Are you listening to me?'

'Yes,' Joe lies. 'What?'

'Make sure the edges of your hood are snug and tight under the goggles, and get your mask in up under there too. You don't want your skin exposed. They give a nasty filthy bite when they're defending their food.'

'Food?'

'The corpse.'

'Right...'

'Head in the game.'

When they're fully suited up and covered from head to toe in protective white plastic, Hagan says, 'It's going to be dark in there, so we need these,' and pulls two head torches from his kitbag, fixing one to Joe's large hooded head before fixing the other one to his own. 'We're good to go.'

Joe's breathing quickens in a way that it might get away from him like a beach ride donkey breaking into a gallop with a screaming fat kid clinging on to its back and everyone on the beach laughing at him.

Hagan sees the panic rising in his padawan's eyes but doesn't feed into it. The best cure for most ills in life is work. 'Take two heavy-duty bodybags and a stretcher and follow me.'

Joe gets busy, taking his mind off his out-of-control internal organs and focusing on the exterior world, making physical decisions that help him feel in control of his environment.

The pair of bodymen make their way into battle.

The head of the technical bureau comes out of the house, removing his mask and sucking in fresh air. 'It's upstairs. On your left as you enter. Heavily infested. The corpse is decapitated. We haven't located the head. Visibility is shit. You might want to have a search around for it. You'll need something to cut cable ties.'

Hagan nods and readies his docket book. 'Do we have a name?'

'The house belongs to a Harry Murphy. May or may not be his corpse.'

'I'll put it in as a John Doe. Who pronounced?'

'Doctor Hall.'

'On scene?'

'The boss is taking this one on.' The technician nods over to one of the detective's cars. 'DCI Sutton.'

Hagan writes the name into the docket book and reads the uncomfortable look on Gallagher's face as she explains something to her boss. He says to Joe, 'Let's get in then.'

Joe is in turmoil again. His mind and body are in complete agreement that he should not be going into this dark house, into this deafening fly hum, into this suffocating stink. But there is some part of his brain that is independent of fear, a part that has control over his arms and his legs that is doggedly sticking to the task and following Hagan into the abyss like a soldier might follow his sergeant up and over the top of the trench into no man's land and certain death.

The bodymen enter into an enormous black cloud of chaotic carrion flies living their best life feeding and fucking and increasing their numbers tenfold every ten minutes. The combined putrid gases of hydrogen sulphide, methane, cadaverine and putrescine emanate from the ripe corpse in the putrefaction stage of rotting somewhere in the darkness of the fly kingdom. The stink sears the air and quickly penetrates Joe's mask to burn his nose and throat and somehow finds a way through internal canals in his sinuses to his eyeballs to burn them too. His eyelids blink rapidly to get the water from his eyeballs like windscreen wipers at full speed in a torrential deluge.

Hagan purposefully encouraged the fly infestation when he left the back door open after his murder here. A fresh corpse can be detected miles away by the carrion fly that will arrive within minutes of the death. Even one lone fly can begin the colonisation of the corpse because they carry their offspring in or on their body to immediately larvae post or posit their produce into the ripe flesh. In a matter of hours, larvae will turn to fully formed maggots, feed, grow, and hatch as new flies to start their life cycle and produce thousands of ravenous offspring. In a single day they can multiply to tens of thousands and in two days to hundreds of thousands. This corpse has been colonised and harvested for most of the week. The fly numbers are now uncountable.

Joe starts to make loud heaving and gagging noises like an old diesel tractor engine trying to start on a cold morning.

Hagan illuminates him with his head torch beam that cuts through the swirling black cloud. The mask makes him sound like Darth Vader. 'Do not take off your mask to puke. They'll be in your mouth and up your nose in a flash.'

Joe holds up his hand to signal that the impending puke is under control.

Hagan knows the layout of the black interior from his previous visit and turns his head toward the stairs. His beam swoops across the wall of flies, and he leads the way into the buzz-hum of darkness. Their combined beams hardly make a dent into the gloom as they climb the stairs in the blind hope that each foot finds a step to stand on. On they go until they are up on the mezzanine. Joe's boots stick to the floor with a crunch, making a boot print like an astronaut making his first small step on an alien planet, its surface matted in a bottom layer of congealed blood that is crusted over by a crunchy top layer of dead flies, their countless corpses glisten in his light.

Hagan can tell by the size and ferocity of the fly cloud that these are probably the fifth or sixth generations to have been born and bred from the corpse.

As the bodymen approach the centre of the flesh fly universe where the headless corpse is decomposing, a wave of flies attack them and begin frantically scouring their protective suits, looking for a breach in their personal protective wear's defences.

Joe falls into a pit of deep despair, manifesting more fear inside his already fear-crammed body.

But there is no real bite in these flies because they have never had to work for their living, never been out in the world, grafting for it. They've never had to fight for their portion of a flat dead crow on the road or a heap of cow shite, or dog shite or any kind of shite for their dinner. All these flesh eaters know is the easy life on the sweet meat of a human corpse that is rich in fat and sugar. However, while they have no bite to them, they do possess the instinct of a true parasite, and they know how to cling to their host. Joe knows they can smell his tasty human flesh, sweating buckets of juicy body gravy inside his forensic suit as he watches a gang of them land on his goggles and look in at him like he's meat in the deli counter, telling each other that he looks really nice. He hears the pitter-patter of hundreds more of them landing on his hood, covering his head entirely in a big black fly ball. His skull warms up, and his brain swims in the buzzing heat. His hands and feet go numb. His ears pound. His eyes sting. His throat is closing up with the sudden onset of tonsillitis because his immune system is kicking into overdrive, as his tonsils go flat-out, preventing germs from entering the body through the mouth and the nose.

While Joe stands covered in flies and wrestles with his out-of-control thoughts, creating a world of horror around him, Hagan moves on through the dense fly cloud until he reaches the far wall. Then, using his hand to blindly search, he finds the window blacked out with a heavy curtain of flies and runs his hand along the frame until he feels the handle and opens it. Whoosh! A sharp blast of fresh mountain air cuts through the stink, hits him in the face, and he loads up on good oxygen.

Not a single fly goes out of the window. Why would they?

Hagan approaches the black writhing cocoon that is a fly-ball consuming the headless corpse sitting cable-tied on a chair in the centre of the room. Removing the box-cutting blade from his pocket, he slowly kneels by the hungry swarm, gently reaching into it, easing through the hot vibrating mass until he finds the plastic strip of cable tie around the torso of the corpse and cuts it, causing it to move slightly... the flies momentarily stop buzzing. He stops. In the white beam of his head torch, he can see the heavy maggot infestation under the blue writhing flesh crawling hungrily out of the torn skin to explore his gloved hand. Then, deciding he's not a threat, the fly hive begins to buzz and go about their business again.

'Give me one of the bodybags here,' he says.

Joe is halfway through his nightmare, wherein he is half fly and half man wandering the empty earth. His hands are two fly balls. It looks like he's wearing boxing gloves as he hands over the bodybag.

Hagan opens the heavy-duty bodybag and spreads it out on the sticky floor. The flies figure out that someone is coming to take their carrion and their millions of maggoty offspring feeding and growing inside of it. When the fly alarm is raised, the buzz-humming increases in volume. Some of the flies start to kamikaze attack Joe's face, bouncing off his goggles, and others start swarming his mask, desperately searching for a way in. They instinctively know that the route into the interior of any animal is through its ears, nose, mouth and anus. These flesh flies have been devouring carrion since the beginning of time and know a thing or two about defending their food, about how and where to bite.

Hagan prepares to move the remains. But Joe has gone on his holidays over to the window. Not too many flies on him now. In his story he has become the King of the Flies. They obey his commands. Eat Hagan instead of me, he tells them. He looks at Hagan, who looks like a human-shaped fly.

'Joe!'

'Yes?'

'What are you doing?'

'Waiting.'

'Waiting for what?'

'Dunno.'

'Get over here.'

166

Joe returns to the battlefield. The flies attack him en masse immediately. The assault intensifies so that the fly force feels like a wave of water hitting him. He panics. 'Fuck.' He swipes out at the black cloud.

'Don't swipe at them.'

He stops. 'But.'

'That just makes them go more mental. Calm down. Do everything slowly.'

'I think one of them got inside me hood.'

'It didn't.'

'What if it gets in me ear?'

'You're grand.'

'It could get into me brain.'

'It won't.'

'Can I go outside and check.'

'No. You do the feet. C'mon.'

Joe moves to the foot end of the great black ball of flies. 'What about the chair?'

'Never mind the chair. The body will slide right off of it. Listen. Are you listening to me?'

Joe nods.

The fly noise becomes deafening.

'The skin will probably be mush, but just grip through it to the bone. Tight. We'll only get one go at doing this right. Okay?'

Joe nods. The flies are now blocking out most of the vision on his goggles, and the buzz-hum of those cocooning his hooded head is deafening and turning his brain to mush.

'But when we lift – be slow. It's bloated and full of maggots, and we don't want to burst it – you got it?'

'Yes.'

'They will kick off. But do not drop it.'

Joe grabs the shins. As he applies pressure to his grip, decomposed tissue and maggots squirt through his fingers as if reaching into a bowl of jelly and custard and trying the take a fistful. It seems impossible to get a grip until he hits the bone, rigid, unmoving, and he knows he's got a hold of the bare shins.

Hagan slides his gloved hands under the armpits, and his fingers find the rib bones for grip. 'On three. One. Two. Lift.'

The moment they lift the corpse, the carpet of flies evacuate it in an explosion and form an angry vortex to drive the thieves away, making kamikaze dives and bombing runs in a sustained assault on the bodymen. A fly storm. The pair carefully move the bloated corpse that shimmers blue and purple like silk in the light from their head headlamps, its bloated body full of writhing maggots that are now desperately trying to break through the skin and escape. A larva will not stay on anything that moves. They know that carrion should be perfectly still. Hagan knows by the swirling motions under the skin that the larvae are now evacuating the corpse, and it is only a matter of seconds before they find accessible exits.

No sooner have they landed the corpse in the bodybag when the first waves of franticly wriggling breakouts appear quickly oozing en masse from the hole where the head used to be. Hagan zips up the bodybag. 'We're going to lift the bag and bring it down the stairs to the hall and put it in the second bag. Right?'

Vomit is creeping up into Joe's mouth now, and his whole body is ready to give it up. He wants out of here. He grabs his end of the bodybag. Hagan grabs the other end, and they haul it down the stairs to the hall under relentless bombardment, place it into the second bodybag and zip it up, then pick up the stretcher and move out. The flies do not follow them out of the house.

The fresh air is like a plunge into the refreshing cold sea. Joe feels a jolt of life come into him as they carry the corpse to the ambulance.

The technical officer joins them. 'Any sign of the head in there?

'No,' says Hagan.

Hagan puts the John Doe tag on the bag's zipper and deposits the remains into the back of the ambulance.

The bodymen then begin peeling out of their filthy forensic suits. As they carefully place the suits into a large biohazard bag, Detective Chief Inspector Sutton approaches them with Gallagher. 'Well done,' he says. 'Not a job for everyone, is it?'

Hagan nods. 'Not a job for anyone, but it's a job that has to be done.'

'Indeed,' agrees Sutton. 'The tech lads said they couldn't get close enough to the body to make any kind of examination. So it's going to be all done in the morgue.'

Gallagher says, 'I can–'

Sutton holds his hand up to stop her talking and says to Hagan, 'If you can make sure that all reports will come back to me.'

Gallagher turns a whiter shade of pale.

Hagan says to Sutton, 'I already have you logged in as the on-scene contact.'

Gallagher says to Sutton, 'Maybe I should go in there and have a search for–'

Sutton cuts her off. 'I don't want anyone going in there apart from the forensic team who will make entry once the flies clear.' He looks to Hagan. 'Usually takes an hour after the body is removed, I'm told.'

Hagan says, 'Less even if the window and doors are opened up.'

Sutton nods. 'I'll get you an escort to the morgue.' He looks to Gallagher, 'You can see to that, can't you?'

'Yes, Chief.' She looks at the uniforms looking on from a safe distance and calls out, 'I need an escort.'

The half dozen uniformed gardai who are present stare blankly at her.

Gallagher asks, 'Is everyone gone deaf?'

A young garda holds his finger in the air to speak.

'What?'

He says, 'None of us have the permit to drive on blue lights.'

Gallagher thinks about a lot of things she could say about that, but her boss is watching her, so she doesn't say anything derogatory about the management of the force. She says, 'I'll do it myself.' She gives Hagan a cutting look, walks to her car and points at the young garda who spoke up, 'You're with me. Now.'

The young garda runs to join her in the car.

The press cameras go into a feeding frenzy as the Gallagher leads out the ambulance with all the bells and whistles going and then floors it up the road, making no effort to wait for the ambulance.

Joe hangs on for dear life as Hagan boots it down the narrow country lane, keeping up with Gallagher, who's burning the tyres off her unmarked Garda car, until they reach the M50 motorway, where Hagan can relax with his foot to the floor and travel in a straight line behind Gallagher who's parting the traffic like a murderous Moses.

Joe watches in amazement as the speed dial goes as far as it can go.

Hagan says, 'Break out those bullseyes from the glove box.'

Twenty diesel and bullseye-sucking minutes later, Hagan enters the security gates at the morgue into the car park.

Kunis is waiting at the bike shed and smoking the last of her cigarette.

Hagan positions the ambulance, gets out, and tells her, 'Maggots.'

'Fuck.'

'Lots of them.'

'Fuck.' She looks at Joe, 'How bad was it?'

Joe keeps on sucking on his bullseye and trying to be cool. 'Doesn't have ahead.'

She reads him and smiles. 'Real fucking bad.'

Joe breaks an involuntary smile. Yes, it was really bad, and he fucking stuck it out and didn't run away with a fly phobia.

She punches him in the arm.

He pretends it didn't hurt.

Everybody who works in the morgue hates maggots. Even as Hagan unloads the double-bagged corpse, he can see movement indicating to him that they have already escaped the first bodybag.

Gallagher arrives at the back of the ambulance, doing her best not to show her hand to Hagan. 'Is there any chance I can have a look at the corpse?'

Kunis flatly says, 'No.'

Hagan adds, 'We can't open those bodybags while the maggots are active.'

Gallagher asks, 'So when will he be examined?'

Hagan looks to Kunis.

Kunis says, 'Well first must get corpse into the fridge. Begin the cooling process. Will kill most of the maggots before they escape. Hard bastard ones the cold does not kill, they get … how you say it?'

'Torpid,' says Hagan.

'That word,' Kunis says. 'Then can be vacuumed away. Thinking maybe noon tomorrow, we give him post-mortem examination. But without head it is hard to say cause of death.'

'Why is that?' Gallagher asks.

'Maybe he is shot in head, and then they decapitate body and take head away to fuck with us.'

Gallagher thinks and then looks at Hagan, but she doesn't ask the question that's burning in her.

Hagan knows she suspects that he dug out the connection between Harry Murphy and Molly's death. And if that is indeed the case, then she can assume that he got the names of the three men who raped Molly the night she died. And if she can establish that much, then Hagan would be the prime suspect for the murders of Harry Murphy, Jeffery Chase and Marcus Strauss – murders that he expertly staged. And if all of that is true, then she would assume that DJ Dennis Doyle is next on Hagan's kill list.

But the problem with a hunch is that it is just that: a hunch. There's no evidence. If she went to her boss to ask for a warrant to arrest Hagan, he would laugh at her and give her some time off to recover from her mental breakdown.

Hagan doesn't budge under her eye.

Gallagher realises that she might be looking at a murderer who knows more about crime scenes than she does, or anyone else does, for that matter. She breaks away. 'Well. I'll let you get on with it. She calls the young garda from her car and says, 'You're on point duty.'

The young garda looks horrified, 'I'm off in an hour, Sergeant.'

Gallagher says, 'You'll be here all night. Think of all the overtime.' And she gets into her car.

'But I don't know what to do. I don't have the training.'

'This is the training. They'll show you what to do.'

Gallagher drives away.

The young Garda looks like a child abandoned at the orphanage.

Hagan knows Gallagher won't rest on her hunch. It will eat her up inside. She'll dig around and go over it all. But it won't matter because he has made a perfect plan to kill DJ Dennis tonight. He wheels the remains of Harry Murphy into the morgue and asks the young Garda, 'What's your name?'

'Conor Keogh.'

Hagan says, 'Welcome to the morgue, Conor.'

'Thanks…'

Hagan tells Joe, 'Bring Conor into the kitchen and make him a cup of tea.'

Joe realises that he is no longer at the bottom of the food chain here; there is someone who knows even less than he does. He relishes taking the rookie Garda through the environs of his domain and showing him where the tea and biscuits are, but not where the kitkats are. That information is privileged.

# CHAPTER TWENTY

HAGAN TURNS OFF the lights of his car as he drives slowly onto the building site of a house renovation high up on the cliff of Killiney Hill. There's not much chance of kids stealing wood from the site, so the builder hasn't bothered to waste his money on a night security guard. The fine house, when completed, will have the much sought-after view of Dublin Bay. For now, it offers Hagan the perfect observational point to the home of DJ Dennis Doyle below. Parking up, he opens his flask of tea with some sandwiches and settles in with his binoculars to observe his quarry. It was too early to make entry into the house, but he wanted to get here with time to spare and prepare for his kill. It's the one thing that Orla The Hitwoman was adamant about. *Give yourself the gift of time.*

'It's beautiful up here, isn't it?' Molly says.

'It is.'

'What do you see?'

Hagan scans the large windows at the back of the house. The curtains are pulled. 'Strange.'

'What's strange?'

'Curtains are pulled.'

She nods her head. 'Last two times we were here, they were open.'

'They were.' He moves his view across the back of the house and to the parking area. 'A garda squad car.'

'Gallagher must have put him under protection.'

'That's plan A gone out the window.'

173

She smiles. 'You always say that there are no problems, only solutions.'

He smiles. 'I do say that a lot, don't I?' He sips his tea and thinks.

After a few moments, she asks, 'Mam is coming back from Spain then?'

'In a few days. I don't think it's good news.'

'No?'

'She said she wants to talk.'

'Talk about what?'

'If I had to guess, I'd say a divorce.'

She goes quiet. He continues to monitor the house, trying to devise a plan B.

An hour later, the security lights at the front gate spark to life, and the gates open automatically as the chauffeur arrives in his sleek black Mercedes. DJ Dennis comes out, gets into the car, and it drives away. The Garda car stays put on point duty. Hagan's plan B comes to him perfectly and fully formed.

# CHAPTER TWENTY-ONE

IT'S DARK AND windy. Hagan waits in the garden of a modest semi-detached house, holding a two-foot length of steel scaffolding pipe in his gloved hands.

David Pike is the perfect chauffeur: fifty, fit, single, ex-army, immaculate, neurotically punctual, discreet and loyal. All good qualities for a man in his position, but he has them all to a fault. It's his discretion and loyalty to his employer that's made him complicit in Molly's death. He wasn't initially on Hagan's kill list, but when DJ Dennis ramped up the security on his home, Hagan was forced to come up with a new plan as to how to kill him, and Pike became part of that new plan. Of course, the plan for Pike is a plan of its own. Hagan tracked him down by the licence plate on his limo, but after some surveillance, he learned that Pike is a naturally cautious man who doesn't leave many things to chance. The garage, which protects his immaculate S-Class Mercedes, and his detached house are fitted with alarms. So, breaking in wasn't an option. It was his neurotic punctuality that presented Hagan with a small window of opportunity.

Monday to Friday, Pike picks up DJ Dennis at five in the morning and takes him to the broadcasting studio. He leaves his garage at four fifteen to give himself plenty of slippage time. But before he sets off for work, he comes into the garage at four o'clock to polish the beloved car with a shammy cloth. After the ten-minute shine session, he allows himself to indulge in his one vice: a cigarette. As part of his ritual, while he's smoking, he opens the garage door to let the air in and the smoke out and stands just outside the garage door to blow the smoke into the sky. This morning, as he steps out of his garage to enjoy his smoke, he is aware of movement in the peripheral vision, and in the next instance, his brain has entered traumatic shock from a blunt force trauma to the head. Maybe his eyes have registered a man in the darkness dressed in a black suit with a white shirt and black tie – like a chauffeur.

After delivering the single blow to the head with the scaffolding pole, Hagan watches Pike standing motionless, staring at him with the blank eyes of a corpse. He waits a moment with the length of pipe cocked over his shoulder and ready to deliver another blow if need be. But it's not needed. Pike's legs fold under him, and his body collapses in a heap like a stringless puppet, slumped in a pile of limbs on the ground where it pants in short, desperate, unregulated breaths like a dog that has been running hard. The brain is in crisis and unable to control the respiratory system. Hagan reaches into Pike's pocket, removes his phone and holds it in front of Pike's face. The phone recognises mapped geometric shapes of its owner's face but has no way of knowing if the face is alive, dying or dead, so it gives access to the phone and its settings. Hagan disables the security features and puts the phone in his pocket.

Next, taking a plastic bag from his backpack, he carefully covers the injured head with it, fixing it in place with a cable tie around the neck, taking care not to make it too tight and leave telltale ligature marks. The head sucks and blows fast, making snapping sounds as it rapidly inflates and deflates the bag and suffocates.

While all that is going on, Hagan sets about the rest of his business, getting the car's fob key from Pike's coat pocket, opening the back doors, changing the door lock settings to child-proof, and covering the inside of the boot with bin bags.

All that done, he returns to the body that is now a resting corpse, takes the bagged head in his gloved hands, cupping one hand under the chin and the other under the base of the skull, and that way, he drags the body along the floor to the back of the car. Moving the body into a sitting position on the floor and looping his arms under the armpits, he heaves the torso up and into the boot. His back screams holy blue murder at him. He takes a moment there and waits for the pain to subside. His lower back starts to lock up. He leans against the wall and uses it to help him straighten himself up through the all-consuming pain, and then pops a few painkillers, closing his eyes as he chews the bitter pills and waits for the opiates to hit the bloodstream and do their work. After a moment, the back-locking pain is subdued to an acceptable level. A cold sweat comes over his entire body, and the pain eases its grip.

'Don't take too many,' Molly says from the garage door. 'They'll make you drowsy.'

'I know.'

He takes a handkerchief, wipes the sweat from his face, and feels his eyes burning. He knows his biggest problem here is dehydration. Every chauffeur carries a supply of bottled water in the boot of the car. Hagan finds Pike's stash, cracks open a small bottle of water, consumes it in one go, and puts the empty bottle back into the boot with the body, making a mental note to take it away with him when his business is done.

Molly stands at the back of the car and looks into the boot at Pike's body. 'He's already gone.'

'Gone?'

'Yes.' She looks at Hagan. 'Time is ticking.'

'Yes.' Returning to the front of the house to get Molly's scooter that he used to travel from his car to the scene, 'This is a great little invention,' he folds it up and puts it into the boot next to the body. 'I think that's everything…'

'You think?' Molly says, 'You need to be sure.'

Going through his mental checklist, he wishes he'd written it all down in his notebook. Usually, he does, but Holly Hitwoman advised him not to leave a paper trail. He takes Pike's phone from his pocket and texts DJ Dennis: *Something came up. Will explain later. I have a man to cover for this morning.* That done, he drives the limousine out of the garage, pressing the garage clicker to close it behind him. The first part of his plan is now completed. Next stop – pick up the DJ Dennis Doyle and kill him.

Molly sits in the passenger seat, watching the coastline glide by below as they make the drive up into Killiney Hill. 'It's very smooth, isn't it?'

'Beautiful car,' he says. 'Pleasure to drive.'

She turns a gold coin in her hand.

'What's that?'

'They call it Danegeld.'

'Right.'

'They have cartloads of it.'

'The ancients?'

'Yes. And they said they have a great bounty for you.'

'Me? For what?'

'For honouring their blood.'

He thinks about that. 'What will happen when I've done DJ Dennis?'

'They will take him like they did the others. Your bounty will be huge and waiting for you.'

'I mean here in this world. With you … and me.'

She shrugs. 'I don't know. Why do you ask that?'

'I thought, you know, once they were all punished that you would, I don't know, go somewhere.'

'Go where?'

'I've no idea.'

'Neither do I.' She looks out of the window again. 'I like it here.'

'Good. I like you being here.'

'I want you to convince Mam to move back into the house.'

'That might be … I think she has her heart set on selling it and getting a divorce.'

'No, she doesn't. She just can't be in the house. Or she thinks she can't.'

'Maybe you could, you know, speak to her.'

'I've tried.'

'You could try again.'

'I could. But you have to try, too.'

'I will. I promise.

It's still dark. He brings Pike's limousine to a stop in front of the high-security steel gates to Dennis Doyle's property and is immediately lit up by a floodlight. The ever-hyperalert security camera perched on the pillar twitches like it has a nervous tick, and a red scanning laser blinks in the iris of its eye as it nervously surveils the car. But the robotic sentinel is not interested in the human that's driving the car. It's communicating in its own language with its own kind, with the small communication device placed into the car's windscreen that makes a high-pitched beep as the self-automated security system pings it. The program inside a computer in the house instructs the hydraulic machine fixed to the gate to open it for the car to enter. It doesn't understand subterfuge. If you have the correct codes, you can kill whoever you like.

Inside the property, the Garda car is parked up in the corner of the crunchy gravel carpark, and the Garda snoozing in it is jolted awake by the exterior floodlights jumping to life in a blinding flash. The Garda peers out into the light and gives a wave to the limousine. Hagan waves back and continues to drive up to the door of the house. The old stone walls surrounding the grounds come into view, revealing that they have been topped off with prison-camp barbed wire.

'This is awful what they've done to this lovely old house,' Molly says.

'This is what fear looks like,' he says. For a moment, he considers driving away again and leaving DJ Dennis to stew in his self-made hell for a few more weeks, but he doesn't have the luxury of time. Gallagher is no doubt going over case notes related to Molly's death, and it will only be a matter of time until she comes to the files in the coroner's office that show the name of Harry Murphy as being the person who made the emergency call. She will then get a warrant to access the computer system and see Hagan's activity in tracking down Murphy. She'll have enough to get her warrant to arrest him for questioning. He doesn't mind going to prison, but he doesn't want to be inside if one of the men responsible is still alive.

'You can see how beautiful it was.' she says, admiring the property, which, like many of its neighbour's properties, was built by the Victorian English who had quarried the mountain for forty-two years to make the great harbour of Dunleary and fell in love with the splendid view.

Hagan drives the car up the gravel driveway, positioning it outside the front door, and waits. DJ Dennis skips out of his house, jumps into the back seat, and says, 'Morning...', looks at Hagan, and asks, 'Did David give you anything for me?'

'He was taken ill, sir. I'm covering for him.' He drives away.

DJ Dennis makes a snarky nod like he's an angry bird trying to peck at Hagan. 'I know that. But did he give you anything to give to me?'

Hagan can tell that DJ Dennis is strung the fuck out, and he knows what he's asking him about. 'I've to pick it up later and bring it to you at the studio.'

DJ Dennis sniffs and pops a few pills. 'You know the drill then?'

'I do, sir. I've been fully briefed.'

'I need that delivered before I go on air.'

'I'll get it done, sir.'

'Good.' DJ Dennis then sighs and delves into his laptop. If he were a better person, he might send Pike a get-well text that Pike would not reply to, and he might then realise the rouse. But he is not a better person. Hagan exits the gate and sets off along the road with his quarry. The Garda car stays on point duty at the house.

Molly sits staring at D.J. Dennis. 'They're waiting for him.'

Hagan gives her a sideways glance.

She says, 'They've allowed Pike to go to where he needs to go. But they will keep this one. They will never let him go. They'll keep him with Strauss and Chase in the oubliette. One for each of them to be forgotten in.' She looks at DJ Dennis and says, 'You will know true oblivion.'

DJ Dennis looks up from his laptop, 'Did you say something?'

Hagan says, 'No, sir.'

Molly says, 'He can sense me here. He's going to freak out soon. You better hurry up.'

DJ Dennis looks out of the window and sees that they are going the wrong way. 'What way are you going?'

'There's roadworks going on down at Colimore Harbour. It's best to go this way to avoid them.'

DJ Dennis looks out of the window, not entirely sure where he is. 'Right...'

Hagan swings off the road and onto the building site.

'What are you doing?'

Hagan drives to the scaffolded building perched on the edge of the cliff, stops, and puts on a pair of gloves.

'I said, what are you doing!' DJ Dennis tries to open the door of the car to get out. 'What the? What the hell?'

Hagan looks back at him, makes eye contact, and tells him. 'I'm Molly's father.'

DJ Dennis goes whiter than a corpse in pallor mortis and starts to dial his phone. Hagan reaches over and takes it from him. He is surprised by how feeble the man's grip is. He can tell that there's not an ounce of strength in his soft jelly body. DJ Dennis gets a dose of verbal scutters. 'That had nothing to do with me. I swear it.'

Hagan gets out of the car, opens the back door and takes the whimpering fucker out by the scruff of the neck. 'Out you come, fucker.'

The fucker pukes, shits, and talks at the same time. 'I didn't do anything. It was fucking Strauss and Chase. I swear.'

Hagan drags the fucker by the scruff of his fuckin neck to the back of the car, where the fucker sees Pike's body. He shits himself at full speed with loud scuttery farts and turns into a limp bag of shit. When he sees Hagan remove a length of scaffolding pole, he starts to pass out.

'Come on, fucker.' Hagan drags him to the edge of the scaffolded building site that spills down the hillside for a hundred yards onto rocks. 'Look at me, you fucker.'

The fucker keeps his eyes closed tight. 'No. Please.'

'Fucking look at me.'

'Please...' He squints open his eyes and looks at Hagan. 'I swear, I was–'

Hagan executes a blow to the fucker's head, killing him like an animal. 'Fucker.' He waits until he feels the body slump in a dead weight. Then he throws the corpse over the edge of the cliff into the mesh of scaffolding works below, where it hits any number of scaffolding poles on its journey, striving to reach terminal velocity, getting well and truly fucked up before it smashes upon the exposed bedrock.

He returns to the car and hauls Pike's corpse out of the boot. His spine should be in unbearable pain, but he doesn't feel a single thing because he is in a flow state, a state of ecstasy like an artist lost entirely in the creation of his masterpiece.

After he's removed the bag from the head, he throws Pike's corpse over the cliff edge, and it also gets well fucked up, hitting the scaffolding on its way down the cliff to join the other fucker's fucked-up corpse.

The dawn chorus begins. He is filled with sudden euphoria, and in the next moment, he is spent. He falls to his knees. 'I'm done,' he says to Molly, but she is gone... He is alone.

The pain of his body returns and grows and begins to swallow him. He reaches into his pocket, takes the last six painkillers from the foil pack, and eats them. For a time, and he's not sure how long, he stays where he is … perfectly numb, almost lifeless, watching the new day break and listening to the birds sing.

His phone vibrates in his pocket, and habit takes over. He answers it, 'Hagan.'

Kunis says, 'Can you come in early?'

'What's wrong?'

'The B team are tied up on a job. We need you to cover an urgent state case.'

'On my way.' He hangs up. A State Case is a sudden death that the State Pathologist judges to be a homicide on the scene of the crime. He gets to his feet, returns to the car, removes the plastic lining and empty water bottle from the interior and puts them into his backpack. Then, closing and locking the car, he sends the key fob, Pike's phone and DJ Dennis's phone over the cliff's edge. Using Molly's scooter, he leaves the scene and returns to his car, parked at the end of the road. Putting the scooter into the boot, he drives to work.

# CHAPTER TWENTY-TWO

IT'S HEAVY RAIN. Joe looks out of the window in amazement. 'Seven garda cars?'

Hagan brings the ambulance through the muddy path and the crime scene tape and along a tight turreted lane to a derelict farm at the back of the airport.

Joe says, 'I bet you it's the missing girl.'

Hagan brings the ambulance to a halt at the entrance to a large dilapidated barn. A dozen technically suited forensic officers comb the area. State Pathologist Dr Cullen comes to the ambulance. 'We've already bagged the body, so you just need the gurney.'

Hagan nods and watches her walking back inside the barn.

Joe makes to speak but Hagan holds up his hand to stop him. 'From this point on, neither of us have anything to say.'

Joe nods.

The pair of morgue men wheel the gurney through the muddy ground into the large open barn that's lit up with a string of halogen crime scene lamps. Here and there, the roof is missing, and the rain pours in to form puddles. A masked technical officer says, 'Avoid these if you can,' pointing to a number of bullet cartridges on the ground that have been marked with bright yellow forensic tags and circled with chalk.

Hagan nods and guides his gurney further into the crime scene. Obviously a gang shooting, he thinks, and he knows that Gallagher will be here. Ahead of him, a body in a bag waits on the ground. It's not a child's body.

Cullen says to Hagan, 'Don't worry about the lift. They want to do it themselves.'

Hagan stands back, and the technical team lift the bagged body onto the gurney. As Hagan and Joe wheel the remains back to the ambulance, the rest of the gardai on scene form into two lines, making a guard of honour. Hagan realises that it's one of their own in the bag, and he searches the faces for Gallagher.

As he loads the gurney into the back of the ambulance, Cullen comes to him. 'You want to fill out your docket?'

Hagan gathers his thoughts and retrieves his morgue docket book, opening it under his coat to keep it from the rain. He can smell perfume now and wonders if it is coming from Cullen or the corpse in the bag.

Cullen says, 'Doctor who pronounced is myself. Deceased name is Helen Gallagher.'

Hagan's hand begins to involuntarily shake as he writes Gallagher's name into the docket.

Cullen sees it and says, 'Sorry. I know you knew her.'

Hagan nods.

'It was quick.'

Hagan nods.

'Let's get her out of here.'

Hagan closes the doors, joins Joe in the ambulance, and waits for the escort. Joe's phone pings, and he reads it. 'It was Danny Boy Delaney.'

'What are you talking about?'

'It's on gangsta rap. They've arrested him for it. Jesus... remember he said to her that he would shoot her in the face?'

'Put your phone away and never, and I mean never, talk about hearing Delaney make that threat.'

Joe nods.

After a few minutes, a six-car escort forms up and speeds the morgue ambulance carrying the body of their fallen colleague away from the crime scene with sirens and lights – cutting through the rain like the chariots of the Valkyrie speeding a fallen warrior from the battlefield.

WILLIAM HAGAN IS Dublin's anonymous Bodyman who arrives
on the scenes of sudden and violent deaths to bag and tag the corpses
and remove them to the City Morgue for a post-mortem
examination. It's a job he's been quietly doing for twenty years,
content in the belief that he's performing a small but important
function in the process of justice and a corporal work of mercy.
  When he turns up on a scene of death to find his daughter's corpse,
all that changes. A year later, his wife has left him, and he lives in an
empty house, sharing his life with the ghost of his daughter, Molly.
There is a reason why Molly's soul is not moving on. The reported
manner of her death as an accident is a lie. Hagan uncovers that she
has been murdered and begins a journey to find those responsible
and punish them. His vast working knowledge of investigative
procedures, pathology and murder enables him to deal with the
guilty undetected.


Declan Croghan is a screenwriter known for creating shows such as
'The Body Farm' for the BBC, 'Life of Crime' for ITV and 'Murder
Prevention' for Channel 5. He's also written multiple episodes of
British primetime television for shows such as 'Waking The Dead'
'Taggart' and 'Ripper Street'.

Printed in Dunstable, United Kingdom

64587447R00107